Once upon a time, a journalist called Rutendo Dione traded in news reporting for the delights of creative writing. Based in Suffolk, she draws inspiration from country walks and the arts, and loves creating thrilling adventure stories with a touch of enchantment.

Presto!

Published in the UK by Sweet Cherry Publishing Limited, 2024
Unit 36, Vulcan House, Vulcan Road,
Leicester LE5 3EF, United Kingdom

Unit 31, The Pottery, Bakers Point,
Pottery Road, Dún Laoghaire,
Dublin A96 EV18, Ireland

2 4 6 8 10 9 7 5 3 1

ISBN: 978-1-80263-086-2

www.sweetcherrypublishing.com

Printed and bound in the UK using 100% renewable electricity
at CPI Group (UK ltd)

MIX
Paper | Supporting
responsible forestry
FSC® C171272

Presto!
Magical Recovery Co.

RUTENDO DIONE

Sweet
Cherry

For Jonathan and Sammy

CONTENTS

Prologue

KIDNAPPED

She appeared out of the sandstorm. The stuff of all children's nightmares, the villain of many a dark story. She hovered above Red, an electrified cloak of multi-coloured stripes crackling and spitting around her. Her waist-long chalk-white hair billowed, a luminescent mane that brushed against deathly pale skin. From a bony, porcelain face, neon-green eyes flashed, spewing hot electric sparks of their own. She smiled menacingly.

The Wicked Witch herself.

'Hello, Little Red Riding Hood,' she rasped, sharp gold teeth glinting. 'Fancy a little trip?'

Dominated by pale moons and never having known a lick of sunlight, the desolate land surrounding them was far from hospitable. The rough terrain was a maze of jagged crystalline rocks and boulders that were difficult to navigate through. The Wizen Plains were an eerie wilderness that most people would be happy to leave as fast as possible. But in that moment Red Riding Hood would have given anything to stay put. Whatever trip the Wicked Witch had planned was sure to be nightmarishly worse.

The Wicked Witch wasn't really asking, though. Whipping up a gale-force wind strong enough to upend any mountain, she whisked Red into her clutches. Red Riding Hood was now a prisoner of the Wicked Witch of the Wizen Plains.

Chapter One

SOCIAL CRIMES

'Stand up straight, darling. Don't shuffle. Remember what I've taught you. No fidgeting. Hands relaxed at your sides. Yes, that's right. Hold your briefcase firmly.'

Relaxed or firm, Mother? You really need to make a choice. Amber sighed, then caught herself. Sighing was yet another unacceptable social crime in her mother's eyes. The list was long – exhaustingly long. Especially when Amber was out in public with her. And right now, her mother had a meeting at Amber's school.

Good old Hampstead Heath, Amber thought. She'd attended the private school since she was five years old – no, scratch that, since she'd been a toddler; there was a preschool attached to the main school. Basically, she'd been at Hampstead Heath School for an age and *then some*! She was basically a thirteen-year-old dinosaur at this point.

Of course, the meeting meant that her mother had insisted that they walk in together – an acute embarrassment. Formally dressed in her two-piece lavender suit, with a tight, straight posture, her mother drew attention. And Amber didn't need any more of that.

As usual, the walk consisted of her mother giving her a full critique of the unacceptable way she had put her uniform together that day. Her tie wasn't straight enough. Her shirt hadn't been properly tucked in. Her shoes could do with more shine. An onslaught of nit-picking that would drive anyone bonkers.

Amber had lived with this ferocious level of fault-finding practically all her life. One would have thought she'd be used to it by now. She wasn't.

Making sure her feet didn't shuffle, while relaxing *and* tightening her grip on her mini briefcase for dear life, Amber wished that the tiled hallway floor would turn into a trampoline and bounce her right up into far-off space. She would fly galaxies away, where there were no measured steps, choking ties or suffocating blazers. No fuss, no frills. No uneasiness constantly slithering through her stomach. And, most of all, no exams.

Just the thought of the upcoming entrance exam was enough to make her heartbeat quicken. This all-important qualifier to the posh boarding school her parents were practically dying for her to get into, had been the dread of Amber's life since she'd started preparing for it. Full-on anxiety threatened to take hold, catching at her throat and tingling in her fingertips. Letting her mother's voice roll over her, Amber concentrated on breathing in and out. She let out a slow, deep exhale of relief when they finally reached the door to her classroom. Lessons would ease some of the anxiety, if only by making her feel that she was working towards what awaited her in a few months.

Of course, her mother hadn't noticed her anxiety.

'Remember, you are due for the Young Ladies' Association appraisal tonight. I won't be home till late afternoon. Make sure to be prepared,' she instructed.

'How could I ever forget?' Amber hadn't meant for the sarcastic tone to creep in. Social crime number two. She was racking them up this morning! Thankfully, her mother let it go without comment. A rarity.

'Also, one of the girls will help you pack for Brixton,' her mother continued, meaning one of the troop of maids she had on express standby at any given time.

Amber groaned. 'Do I really have to go?' The upcoming weekend was going to be the start of the spring break. It felt like the worst kind of punishment to be spending it in Brixton, especially with some random uncle she had only seen a few times over the last couple of years.

'We've been through this before, Amber. Your late grandpa requested in his will that you spend this particular weekend in the old house in Brixton with your uncle.'

'But surely you and Father could come too?' Amber complained.

'Your grandpa specifically stated that it should be grandchildren only. And you're the only grandchild. Plus your father has an important annual meeting in New York, which he can't afford to miss.'

'But–'

'You're going, young lady,' Amber's mother said firmly. 'End of. Now, shoulders straight, and in you get.'

'Okay.' Amber squared her shoulders as she'd been told.

'Good girl.' Her mother proffered a cheek. Careful not to smudge the pristine make-up, Amber quickly kissed her goodbye. She wasn't sure which of them couldn't get away fast enough – herself or her mother.

As usual, there was a bustle of activity inside the classroom. The teacher hadn't arrived yet and kids clustered in groups, messing around or chatting – mostly messing. Mobile phones glued to hands, it was a hive of endless scrolling and screen tapping.

On her way to her seat at the back of the room, another knot of anxiety tightened in Amber's stomach as she caught sight of Katie Marsh. Her ex-best friend. She was huddled with a bunch of other girls, and they were talking over each other at every turn. Silky straight blonde strands were cut into the same shoulder-length style, pale cheeks were made equally rosy with faint blusher and soft lips were stained with the exact same pink lip gloss – they were literal clones of one another.

Amber took a deep breath to steady her nerves. Unfortunately, she would have to squeeze past them to get to her own seat.

'Excuse me,' she muttered. No one seemed to hear her. They were laughing at something Katie had said. Amber shuffled past awkwardly. Letting out another breath of relief, she plonked down in her chair. *There. Done.* To cover up her embarrassment, she also took out her mobile and pretended to text. Relief washed over her as Mr Maguire came in. The friend clusters broke up, and all phones were dutifully tucked away.

Amber eagerly pulled out her laptop. Computer Science was her absolute favourite subject. Top of the class, year after year, the world of computer science was her oasis. She shone in programming – though it was mostly a closely guarded, quiet kind of shine. Amongst the other girls, Amber already stood out (far from fair-skinned, with anything *but* silky hair!), and drawing attention to herself was the last thing she wanted to do.

However, halfway through the lesson, Mr Maguire did the unthinkable. When no one answered his question, he asked Amber directly. Her actual worst nightmare. She knew the correct response straight away, obviously. All she had to do was say it out loud.

As Amber looked up and slowly inhaled, filling her lungs with courage, she accidentally locked eyes with Katie. Bright green eyes pierced her dark brown ones. Amber couldn't speak.

'Right,' Mr Maguire said, after the pause stretched on for far too long, before explaining the concept himself. Katie turned back to her friends, giggling. Amber wished she could just melt into the classroom furniture. What she wouldn't do for the wave of a magic wand right about now! Where were fairy godmothers when you needed them?

Chapter Two

WORST END OF A DEAL

Sitting with her back stiff against the cool leather seat of the chauffeur-driven car, Amber tapped furiously at the keys of her laptop. Just one final input message and the app design would be complete. She'd only been working on it for the last six hours straight.

In three more clicks, she'd have it – the closing data to a software upgrade that she needed.

One.

If she could just get the right algorithm …

Two.

With the interactive interface synced to the gaming app, there'd be a bit of an escape from her upcoming two weeks of torture …

Thr–

'Amber.' Her mother's voice burst through her concentration like a spike puncturing an inflated water balloon. 'Amber, darling?'

Splash. Splatter. Splosh. That was her whole focus draining away. Amber sighed, fingers slackening on the keyboard.

'Yes?' Glancing up, she pushed her thick, coiling fringe of coppery curls from her eyes.

Her mother thrust an illuminated phone screen under Amber's nose. Bright, vividly filtered images scrolled as her mother's manicured fingers flicked nimbly across the display.

'What stunning social pages Katie creates,' she said.

'Lovely girl. I recall a time when you two could never be apart.' More scrolling, more *oohs* and *aahs*. 'It's been an age since she's been round. You two *are* still close?' As usual, her mother didn't wait for a response. 'Of course you are. You've been together since Reception Year!'

Amber stared out of the window. There was no stopping her mother once she warmed to a topic. This was basically their whole dynamic. Her mother talked; Amber listened.

Her father sat across from them in his usual dark business suit and tie. Amber couldn't remember the last time she had seen him in anything else, or without his mobile pressed to his ear. Right now, he was on yet another long conference call. More pressing legal work that just couldn't wait, no doubt. His deep baritone was well-modulated and unhurried as he spoke. Although he'd left Africa with his family as a teenager, there was still the hint of a Kenyan accent there.

'When we all get back to Hampstead, you should have Katie round for a sleepover.' Her mother was still talking.

Yeah, right, Amber thought. She and Katie hadn't spoken in over two years. And now that boarding school was around the corner, it wasn't likely to change. Caught up in camera angles and lighting as a rising social media influencer, Katie hadn't been able to understand Amber's growing fascination with tech, especially the coding aspect of it. One day she'd announced that she 'didn't speak geek', and that had been that.

There was no point even trying to explain this to her mother. She was so preoccupied with her own life – think *The Real Housewives of Hampstead* – and having everything 'just so' was incredibly important to her. A daughter who had been cast aside for preferring geek to chic definitely didn't align with this.

Sighing very quietly to herself, so as not to start another 'crimes against society' lecture, Amber gazed out of the window as Brixton flashed by. Artisan coffee shops nestled next to greasy spoons and grocery stores next to shipping containers full of food markets. It was a different world.

We're not in Hampstead anymore, Toto, she thought, remembering a line from *The Wizard of Oz*, one of her favourite old-time movies. She just wished she had a pair of red shoes to click together and get home.

'Right. Nearly there,' her father announced, putting down his phone and tapping his wristwatch. Amber could see he was impatient to be gone already. It was alright for him. He was off to the Big Apple (of course, her mother had decided to go too. 'Darling, the shops are to *die* for,' she had told Amber). Meanwhile, Amber herself was being ditched at Uncle Randall's, who was practically a stranger. Why did it feel like she'd got the worst end of the deal?

'You have your textbooks?' her father asked, his brown eyes fixed on her like she was one of his employees at the law firm.

'Yes, Father,' she replied dutifully.

'And the preparatory exam papers?'

'Yep. All filed away in my cases.'

'Good. You know how important this exam is for your position at Regency College.'

Yes, Father. I know I've only been provisionally accepted, and it all hangs on how well I do in the entrance exam.

Yes. I'll spend my whole spring break studying.

And, no, I won't dare to even think of taking an actual break or have one single bit of fun. I mean imagine that, Amber Abeiro actually having a good time.

The saddest thing about it all was that Amber couldn't actually remember the last time she had just had fun.

Chapter Three

BIRTHDAY HOUSE

Getting out of the car, Amber looked curiously up at Uncle Randall's bulky grey-brick Victorian townhouse. It stood out from the rest of the terraces in the lane. Five storeys high and wider than them all, it dwarfed anything and everything around it. This was the house her father and uncle had grown up in. Exactly thirty years ago they had moved into it with her grandparents. *Happy birthday, house,* Amber thought. She just hoped her uncle wasn't planning a party. She was not feeling in any way celebratory.

Amber's father had told her that Uncle Randall inherited the house after Grandpa Abeiro passed away. He had turned the building into apartments since then, converting the top floor into his own private apartment.

Amber tried to imagine what it must have been like for her father and Uncle Randall growing up in such a house. Even after all the renovation, it still radiated a sense of wonder. There was clearly a story to tell, each jagged line, crack and crevice seemed to mark a strange and possibly exciting history.

'Make the most of your time here, darling,' her mother called from the car window, carefully shading her face with her hand. She couldn't allow even a glimmer of those harmful rays to touch her naturally bronzed skin. Vampires and Amber's mother had a lot in common.

Bye, Amber. I love you! Would it really kill her mother to utter those few words?

Tightening her grip on her laptop bag, she followed her father across the street to where Uncle Randall was waiting. He immediately scooped Amber up in a massive bear hug – not that Uncle Randall looked anything like a bear. He was just as tall and lanky as she remembered. His keen sense of fashion hadn't changed much either, she noted, as she was crushed against the silken fabric of a sun-reflecting lime shirt, artfully decorated with pictures of constellations.

'Look at you!' he said, stepping away and beaming at her. 'A right little lady you've become!'

Released from the hug, Amber returned her uncle's greeting more sedately. She gave a small smile, taking in the rest of his unique dress style. Every single thing was just as striking as his shirt: bright yellow trousers paired with white embellished designer trainers, and a short crop of jet-black beaded locs styled into a neat box cut on his head.

Amber was suddenly conscious of her own clothes, each stitch specially selected by her mother:

a smart floral dress and neat closed-toe sandals. Preppy elegance. Hardly the cutting edge of self-expression.

Uncle Randall turned to her father. 'Hello, Andy.' He held out a hand. Her father shook it stiffly.

'Randall,' was his full response.

Amber rolled her eyes as they struggled to make conversation, like two strangers forced to talk on a random street, rather than brothers standing outside their childhood home. *Grown-ups*. Millennia could pass and they'd never let an argument go. Amber had heard the occasional whispers about it when her parents spoke. Something to do with their father and a fall out over business? She really didn't know the details. Nor thought too much about it.

After a short, stilted talk with his brother, Amber's father said his goodbyes to Amber. Gruff last-minute reminders followed by a curt nod. Definitely *no* hugs slipping in there. Her parents had never been the touchy-feely types.

As the Rolls-Royce slunk away, carrying her parents into the distance, an upbeat Uncle Randall gave her another hug. *He doesn't seem to have got the touchy-feely family memo*, thought Amber, as she followed her Uncle Randall inside the house.

Amber braced herself for the longest two weeks of her life.

'I'm happy to have you here, Amby,' her uncle said. *Amby*. He was the only one who ever called her that. Amber didn't say anything. Unbothered, he went on energetically, 'We're going to have us a really great time; you can count on that!'

Amber wasn't sure she could count on that at all.

Chapter Four

THE MAGIC
OF SCIENCE

'Welcome, welcome!' Uncle Randall said, lugging
Amber's cases along a carpeted corridor. They had
reached the top floor, which was a secluded lobby
area just outside of his flat. Wallpapered in mosaic
patterns on either side, with gold-plated twin doors

at the very end, the small space dazzled.

'My very own private abode!' Uncle Randall proudly announced, before quickly adding, 'Though visitors are most welcome and always frequent! I find being around a good many people energising. How about you?'

Taking in the high windows and the huge vases shaped like gourds of tropical fruit beneath them, Amber sincerely hoped that these visitors her uncle was so keen on would give drop-ins a miss during her stay. She couldn't bear the thought of random strangers popping up at any minute. She didn't do too well with the unfamiliar or the unexpected, and she liked her own space and privacy. But to Uncle Randall, she said, 'I'm not fussed either way.'

A big flash of white teeth as he smiled. 'Great!' He turned the key in the door and pushed, holding it open for her. 'Welcome, my lady.'

Amber stepped inside nervously. A large living area, wide and airy, lay in front of her. Thick burgundy carpet with an assortment of brightly coloured rugs spanned its entire length, framed with glossy yellow walls that were covered almost entirely in artwork – paintings and crafts alike. In an alcove, heavy green drapes were held back by bronze claws and white laces that fluttered against open windows. There were gold-upholstered armchairs beside a plush blue velvet sofa. And in front of that was the TV. Mounted to a wall adjacent to the fireplace, it stretched tall and long, almost blocking out the entire wall behind it. Even with the busyness of the surroundings, it was instantly eye-catching. Amber had never seen a TV so big.

'Wow,' she breathed. 'That's massive.'

Uncle Randall chuckled behind her. 'All the better to see it, right?'

They went past an office space just as chaotically flamboyant as the living room: books crammed into shelves against the walls, computer monitors and gadgets crammed onto a wide, cluttered desk. Beyond that were two bedrooms. Uncle Randall's was furthest along the hallway, and what would be Amber's was closest to the entrance.

Dropping her case in the middle of her new

room, Uncle Randall finally puffed out a breath. 'You certainly brought enough stuff with you!'

Amber sank down on the double bed, electric blue cushions scattered across the deep maroon velvet duvet cover. An emerald canopy hung over the bed, star-shaped fairy lights dangling across its edges. On the windowsill at the far end of the room, celestial trinkets created a cluster of starry chaos. This place was nothing like home. She could just imagine what her interior-design-mad mother would say about it: *Over-stuffed, over-decorated and downright shabby.* Amber herself couldn't decide just yet if she found it totally horrendous or entirely spectacular. It certainly made a change from the neutral, *fine-taste* décor she'd been subjected to all her life.

'Are these textbooks in here?' With a frown, Uncle Randall tapped one of the overloaded cases where a thick volume stuck out of the partially done-up zip.

'I have a lot of studying to do,' Amber replied, opening her laptop bag. 'First it is going to be

Maths revision. After that, I'll focus on languages, and then after that, I'll be polishing up my spelling and grammar. Then it will be time for the reading lists ...'

Her uncle's eyes were saucer-wide behind his tortoise-shell-framed glasses. 'Really? All that when you're on a glorious two-week break? Surely not!'

Amber saw something flash across his face, something that that looked a lot like pity.

'I have my entrance exam coming up,' she said quickly. 'Mother and Father put a lot into making sure I'm ready. It's been extra lessons with private tutors, professional study plans – everything! I *have* to be ready.'

At this, her uncle seemed thoughtful. 'You've certainly changed since we last saw one another.'

Amber knew this wasn't meant as a compliment. *Does he think I'm just as uptight as Mother?* she thought. It made her shrink back a little. The last time she'd seen him, she'd been much younger, and he'd managed to pry her out of that gloom, prod her to have more fun and not take herself too seriously.

One time, perhaps on her fifth or sixth birthday, he'd bought her a toy unicorn as a gift. It was bigger than her! Together they'd run around town taking turns pretending to ride on it and making up fantastical 'Amber and the Unicorn' stories that were so silly they had almost burst from giggling. At one point, Uncle Randall had ruffled the glittery rainbow mane of the toy animal, treating it as if it were real. 'Remember this, Amber-Ramber,' he had said to her quite seriously – he always called her Amber-Ramber when he got serious. 'There's magic in each of us, waiting to burst free. We just have to let it out.'

But somewhere along the way, Amber had lost that magic. She wasn't a little girl anymore. And she didn't have time for magical creatures or silly make-believe stories. She was sorry if that disappointed her uncle, but that was life. *Yet another person to add to the 'People Amber Has Disappointed' list*, she thought. Suddenly desperate for him to go away, she started up her laptop and began furiously tapping away on it.

'So, I heard you're a coding prodigy now,' Uncle Randall began. 'I still remember teaching you the basics on Python when you were small.'

'Hmmm,' Amber answered, keeping her eyes on her screen and giving off her best 'please leave me alone' body language.

Uncle Randall didn't take the hint. He fussed with her bags and adjusted furniture, like someone on the hunt for something to do. Out of the corner of her eye, Amber saw him repeatedly reach up to his shirt pocket, only to take his hand away each time.

Finally, she couldn't take any more.

'Uncle Randall, are you okay?'

'Hmm? What?'

'You're acting really weird.'

'Er ... no. Not weird. Just ... I'm wondering ...'

'Wondering what?'

Uncle Randall looked at Amber for the longest moment. Then, once again, he put his hand to his shirt pocket. *Seriously, what is this man's deal?* Amber thought. He strode across the room and sat down next to her on the bed.

'Amber-Ramber,' he started, the velvet cover crumpling beneath him. Amber sighed and pushed her laptop aside. Their eyes locked.

Uh-oh, thought Amber. *He's got his serious grown-up face on.*

'There's so much more to life than studying. What if I told you that there are magical realms within our world? You need a sprinkle of magic in your life.'

Amber slowly raised her thick, coppery eyebrows. 'What? Like conjuring bunnies out of hats. Or cutting me in half? No thanks.'

'No, I mean *real* magic,' Uncle Randall replied softly.

'I don't believe in fairy tales anymore, Uncle Randall.'

'Why not? Fairy tales are all around us, you just need to be open to seeing them.'

Yeah, right, and my middle name is Cinderella.

'Okaaaaaaaay,' said Amber. She knew her uncle was a professor of Physics. Maybe he had fumed his brain from too many experiments. Her parents had left her with the dictionary definition of a mad professor.

Her uncle was looking expectantly at her, but she was thoroughly confuzzled. What did he want her to say? That she'd bumped into Rumpelstiltskin in the park?

'Look, Uncle Randall ...'

'Call me Randall. Uncle makes me feel old.'

'Okay ... Randall. Honestly, unless you have magic that will make me remember all this stuff, then I really need to get on.' Once again, she reached for her laptop.

She caught the pursing of his lips, excitement dashed. Just when she was wondering if she should apologise for being rude, he perked up.

'Righto! Settle yourself in then. Have a quick freshen up. We need to hit the road in a few minutes. I have a gig at a local restaurant, y'see. How do you fancy an evening of jazz on the vibey streets of sweet ol' Brix?'

Aside from the recent magic conversation, Amber couldn't think of anything worse.

Chapter Five

NEW LIFE, NEW BEGINNINGS

Amber hurried to keep up with Randall as he strode through the crowded evening streets. She really needed to be getting on with her studies. Her father would have a cow if he thought she wasn't spending every single moment nose-deep in her books. Amber could just imagine what he'd say: 'An utter waste of valuable time!' And for once she had to agree.

Honestly, what did she care about the anniversaries or ridiculous whims of a grandpa she had never known? By the time she'd been born, Andrew Abeiro Senior was long dead and buried. Her father barely mentioned him. All this meant that Amber had only a vague outline of him being the founder of the law firm her father worked for, and what sounded like the very stiff backbone of the family. It seemed heaps unfair to have her stay in Brixton based on some musty old promise that she couldn't care less about.

'Ah! Here we are,' Randall announced, interrupting her spiralling thoughts. 'The famed Keyway Moon!'

Amber looked up at the bright and colourful rectangular building tucked between two shops. 'Famed' had to be a bit of an exaggeration on her uncle's part, the place looked pretty ordinary to Amber.

'After you!' Randall gestured for her to go in first. As Amber stepped inside, she had to swallow her words. This was like no restaurant she had ever been to before. A raised stage took pride of place

42

in the middle of the floor. Patterned wallpaper covered every wall, displaying scenes of an African savannah: long brownish grass, tall trees and bushes surrounding elephants, rhinos, giraffes, zebras and many more. Under the glare of luminous chrome wall lamps, the animals shimmered.

Even more surprising was the sheer number of people squeezed inside. The place was packed. Almost every available seat was taken, with still more people standing in clusters around a bar area at the far end of the room.

Amber followed behind Randall as he squeezed through the crowds towards the stage. It was slow progress; Randall was stopped after almost every other step by people keen to greet him.

'We're seeing you on stage tonight, no doubt?' asked someone.

'Cosmic craters couldn't stop me!' Randall responded, drawing laughter from several people around him.

Amber looked at her uncle in horror. She couldn't think of anything worse than being on stage. She just hoped he wasn't horribly embarrassing.

Another man gave him a quick handshake. 'Please say you're playing *New Life, New Beginnings*?'

'You know it!' Randall replied.

By the time they got to their seats, not only were Amber's feet bruised from so many people accidentally stepping on them, but she was looking at her uncle with fresh eyes. No one here seemed to think he was odd or a mad professor. He treated every single person with kindness, exuding warmth and energy. She was pretty sure this had been one of the reasons she had been drawn to him when she was younger. He was like the sun emerging from behind the dark cloud of her parents.

A waitress in a checkered apron and bright blue headdress, which seemed to be part of the restaurant uniform, placed plates piled with food in front of them. She gave Amber a warm smile, deep dimples in her cheeks. Amber couldn't help grinning back as the spicy scent of the traditional ugali dish made her realise how hungry she was. She cut into the side dish of chicken drenched in mango chutney.

'I give a special performance every Easter,' Randall said, dipping a spoonful of ugali into the chutney. 'It's the rise of the paschal full moon, and it marked three important moments in my father's life: coming to this country, moving into the house and when he died. Different years, of course. Quite a coincidence, hey?'

Amber frowned. 'My Computer Science teacher says if we want to be coders, we have to follow the statistics. And that means there's no such thing as a coincidence. In large populations, any weird event is likely to happen.'

'Hmm,' said Randall. 'That might well be true. But don't let it close your mind to the weirdness and wonder that's all around you, if you're brave enough to look. It's what I like to call the magic of science.'

Please not the magic speech again, thought Amber.

She changed the subject quickly. 'Is this full moon stuff why it's so important that I spend these next two weeks with you?'

'That's exactly right,' Randall confirmed. 'Grandpa Abeiro might not have met you, but he wanted his children, his children's children and of course their children to carry on the family traditions and values.'

Amber's head was starting to spin. 'But I still don't get why it's so important,' she said.

'Your grandpa grew up here, but when he became a young man, he went back to Africa. That's where he met your grandma, fell in love and had a family. We didn't move to the UK until your father and I were teenagers. Being able to buy a home here for his family meant a lot to your grandpa. An immigrant's life is rarely an easy one. And your grandpa was very proud of his roots and what he achieved here.'

Amber nodded. She herself had never felt like an immigrant, being British born, yet a part of her could relate to being different. That feeling of straddling two worlds; a foot in each, but never really part of either. And she had to admit it was nice to be here, in this restaurant and town, where the majority of people were similar in colouring to her and her uncle. It brought about a new but not unwelcome sense of ... belonging. It wasn't just the vibrant intensity of the place or the people with their warmth and openness, it felt like coming back to her roots.

'I get you, Grandpa,' she whispered. She hoped the grandpa she had never met would be proud of her.

Moments later, Randall took to the stage. As he strummed on his guitar, Amber couldn't help but admire not only his ease, but his open enjoyment of the music and performing.

Perhaps these two weeks wouldn't be so bad after all. If nothing else, she'd certainly come to an interesting place, and her uncle was definitely an interesting man.

Chapter Six

A FRIEND
IN NEED

The various pieces of art displayed around Randall's flat seemed infused with a life of their own. Bold and colourful, they were designed to grab attention. They were all different but felt other-worldly. Floating silvery dunes in desert lands, ocean depths with sunken, spired castles, and even towers sitting on top of clouds.

Amber couldn't stop looking at them! And, she had discovered, every single one was the work of her uber-zealous uncle. They were just as buoyant as he was. Amber still hadn't forgiven her parents for ditching her there, but it was hard not to like her uncle. He was an oddball, but then so was she. *Just ask Katie*, she thought.

Amber knew her mother would fly off the handle if she could see her now, sitting on the sofa cramming cereal into her mouth straight from the box. But her mother was in the middle of a grand shopping spree in New York City, so this was a handle-flying-free zone.

She could hear the whirring of the shower still going, as well as her uncle's cheerful humming bouncing off the bathroom walls. It didn't sound like he was going to be finished any time soon. *Why not break yet another of Mother's rules?* Amber thought. No watching TV while eating. She pressed the button on the remote. Nothing happened. Only a dull orange glow came from the huge screen. So much for its razzle-dazzle fanciness – the stupid thing didn't even work!

Disappointed, Amber stood up to turn it off when a weird crackling noise twanged out of the speakers. The orange glow deepened, then brightened. Lighter and lighter until the whole surface seemed enflamed. Transfixed, Amber leaned in closer ...

Out of the screen leaped the biggest, hairiest creature she had ever seen! It was wearing the oddest collection of clothing and stood impossibly tall – its broad shoulders just about scraped the ceiling! Its ebony-black paws were the size of bricks and it flexed thick, fur-coated muscles. Choking back a startled cry, Amber tripped over herself as she tried to get away.

'Hey, steady on!' The creature spoke in a growl that made Amber feel anything *but* steady. 'The Prof. Where's the Prof, lassie? This is urgent.'

Amber could only stare at this talking beast, her eyes wide. Was the creature actually a wolf? But wolves didn't stand upright, did they? Or wear bandit-style clothes? Or *speak*?

Her mind a whirlpool, Amber continued to stare, gobsmacked. It was like something out of a fairy tale. Could it be ...? No, it couldn't be! *Magic?* Was what Randall had said ... *true?* Every last word of it?

Amber blinked. Closed her eyes. Opened them again. Nope. There was no getting around the fact that an actual wolf was standing upright and talking to her in the middle of her uncle's living room.

When three crazy-eyed cubs also dressed in leather vests, gloves and boots leaped out of the screen and stood behind the colossal wolf, Amber finally regained her voice. She let out a screech so loud it could have shattered glass.

'What in the confuddling cosmos?'

Randall stumbled into the living room, dripping wet from the shower. He fumbled with a dressing gown and struggled to straighten his specs.

'Wolf!' he cried.

'Hi, Professor!' The massive creature stepped forwards, causing Amber to let out another involuntary scream and speedily retreat into a corner.

'Uh, you might want to quieten your wee girl there, Prof,' the wolf growled. 'A bit on the loud side.'

'Really, this is unacceptable, Wolf.' Randall tried to adjust his shower cap, dollops of soap still on his face. 'You can't just turn up at my house like this!'

Wolf gave an impatient *harrumph*. 'I'm sorry, Prof, but this is an emergency.'

'Unacceptable. Totally unacceptable.' Randall turned to Amber. 'My dear girl, it's all right. There is nothing to fear, they're friends ...'

Amber stopped screeching and slowly returned from what felt like anaphylactic shock. She focussed hard on slowing her breathing.

'Well, they *were* friends. We may need to revise that.' Randall shot a disapproving look at the trio of cubs now running amok in his living room. Stumpy tails wagging wildly, the raggedy creatures bounced off arm chairs, tabletops – even the walls.

'Hey, don't touch that! No. Don't—'

One of them picked up a vase to try on as a hat.

'Put that down, Beastly,' Wolf growled.

Amber didn't know whether to laugh or cry. *Beastly? Nope. Not weird. None of this is weird at all!*

The slobbering cub lifted the vase off his head, two pointy ears popping out from its rim. This time, Amber let herself giggle.

Wolf was now talking at a furious rate. 'I tried to call; honest I did.' Dusty, heavy boots thudded across the floorboards as he paced around the room. 'I rang and rang, over and over again!'

Thud. Thud.

'Got nothing. No response.'

Thud.

'What was I supposed to do? Red's in a serious pickle. If I don't fix this, I'm done for.'

Thud.

'I'm going to get the chop – the Woodcutter's axe hangs over me for this type of thing!'

Thud. Thud. Thud.

'I shouldn't have agreed to take that little

monster on in the first place. I shouldn't have done it. I shouldn't have–'

'All right, all right.' Randall threw his hands up. 'Stop with the pacing before you bring down the whole building!' Randall skirted past the fidgety cubs to the fireplace. He picked up a spangly watch from the mantel and glanced at it. 'Seventy-seven missed calls. All from you, I take it?' He looked at Amber. 'Amber-Ramber, I'm so sorry about this. Certainly not the way I wanted to introduce you to the constructs of the Hidden Realms of Fairy Tales.'

Amber looked up at him, trying to find the words to express the bafflement mushing her brain. 'How is this even possible?'

A small grin played at the corner of her uncle's lips. 'Remember that magic of science I was banging on about? Physics is a magnificent thing, Amby.'

'But *how*? How did … *they* … come out of *that*?' She pointed at the wolves, then at the still shimmering TV screen.

'We haven't got time for this!' muttered Wolf.

'What part of "emergency" does your wee bairn not understand?'

'All in good time, Wolf,' Randall replied, picking up the remote Amber had dropped earlier. 'This is no ordinary TV controller, my dear. It's fitted with a descriptor, an element that sends signals to that screen over there and makes quantum tunnelling possible.'

'Quantum tunnelling?' Amber was lost again.

'Yes, child.' Randall replied. 'This remote is rooted to the elementary particles of a unique gemstone called Angelpyrite, and creates higher states of energy and vibrations, mechanically tunnelling through the universe's quantum scope to the Hidden Realms – the place our friends here call home.'

'Not for much longer,' came another deep growl from Wolf. 'Gran Red is going to have my hide skinned and exiled if I don't find her precious little Red Riding Hood! So can we get a move on, please!'

'Keep your fur on,' Randall said. 'All good things come to those who wait.'

Letting out a breath, Amber fully faced the strange gigantic creature for the first time. 'Little Red Riding Hood? Are you talking about the character from the story?'

Wolf let out a rumbling laugh. 'He's never been keen on the "little" part, that's for sure.'

Amber's eyes widened. 'Little Red Riding Hood is a *he*?'

Wolf turned to Randall. 'Is she going to keep repeating everything I say? Since when did you have a daughter, Prof?'

'Amber is my niece, Wolf. And a little more courtesy, please. She's new to all this.'

Amber was desperately trying to put the pieces together.

'Hang on,' she said. 'If Little Red Riding Hood is real, then that makes you …'

'Let me give you a clue.' Wolf grinned, revealing two rows of sharp, white teeth. 'All the better to eat you with.'

'You're … You're … the Big Bad Wolf!' Amber turned to her uncle and stared at him. 'But doesn't that mean he *eats people*?' She mouthed the last two words. A wolf who had a granny-eating reputation was the last creature she wanted to offend.

'Both Red Riding Hood and Gran Red are alive and kicking, thank you very much,' said Wolf. 'I'm right reformed, I'll have you know.' He reached out a massive paw to shake her hand.

'Not that much by the looks of things.' Randall snapped on his spangly watch and asked, 'How did you get here, anyway?'

'Desperate situations call for desperate actions. When I rang and there was no answer, I had to take it to the next level, didn't I? Let ourselves into your workshop, helped ourselves to that spare Teleportation Element of yours - and voilà! You really shouldn't leave your stuff just lying around, Professor.'

'*You* really shouldn't be breaking into people's property!' Randall sighed. 'So, what's the deal with Red?'

'He's missing,' Wolf said bluntly.

Amber's head was spinning as she tried to wrap

her mind around what was happening.

Wolf reached a chunky paw inside the purse strapped around his waist and pulled out a small block. He slid it open to reveal a glassy screen illuminated with the scribbly markings of a map.

'Red was doing some work experience for me at Loopy Looters. I owed Gran Red a favour, see. Anyway, Red was gathering metals and minerals from the Plains to sell on. All my workers each have trackers embedded into their scooters, and Red had one on his bike. So when he didn't come back, I tried to find him. But all I'm getting is error codes.'

Amber and Randall peered at the map on the screen. Wolf's furry fingers tapped across it to highlight the information.

'The gang and I tried to track him down – and you know I'm no amateur when it comes to tracking, Prof – but it's as if all traces of him have been wiped clean. The lad's vanished off the face of the Plains!'

'Hmm.' Randall thoughtfully tapped the rim of his spectacles. 'We're going to need heftier equipment for this one. That app of yours has reached its limits, Wolf. But worry not.' He smiled brightly. 'The workshop computers are fitted with top-class frequency modulators and have excellent reach!'

'So you'll be able to find Red?' Amber asked hopefully. She hated the thought of anyone being lost in any way. After all, that was how she had felt for the last few years. She wasn't sure if she even knew who Amber was any more. She was so busy trying to please everyone else.

'I'll do everything I can, Amby,' Randall said, sounding determined. 'And you, my young tech whizz, are going to help me.'

Amber opened her mouth to argue.

'What?' Her uncle nudged her teasingly. 'You'd rather stay at home and study? Amber, my dear, I've never met anyone more in need of adventure in my life. I won't hear another word about it.'

Amber stared at Randall for a minute. She was sick of being told what to do. But maybe, just maybe, this was her chance to see who she was without parental rules and school textbooks. Besides, what could go wrong? All fairy tales had happy endings. Didn't they?

Chapter Seven

BEYOND THE PIXELS

'Ready?' Randall gave Amber a reassuring wink. Thankfully, he was now dry and fully dressed. 'They're not quite what you would imagine, the fairy tale lands – as you've seen here with our friend Wolf and his predicament.'

That's putting it lightly, Amber thought drily. 'It's all so very different from any fairy tale I've ever read!' she replied.

Randall chuckled. 'That's because the fairy tales you know are only the tip of the iceberg, Amby. Folklore, oral histories, traditions, they all come with an idea – nobody could comprehend the full scope of true fairy tale lands. Rumours, stories from people who've seen something, travel across millennia and quantum realms by accident and are built into a mesh. There's more to it all than anyone could possibly imagine.'

Amber thought about this for a moment. 'Like coding, you mean?' she asked. 'Every code you input builds up a mesh too, in a way.'

Randall smiled and nodded. He even looked a little impressed. 'Yes, you're exactly right! It is rather like coding.'

Amber could imagine it – well, almost. The huge screen in the living room blazed in front of her. She'd just watched in disbelief as Wolf and his troop of cubs jumped through the light to the other side. Wherever that might be. And now it was her turn.

She was still trying to make sense of it all. Amber felt like Alice falling down the rabbit hole. Things were certainly getting curiouser and curiouser. The back of her neck tingled with the familiar fingers of anxiety as she inhaled, exhaled - and stepped into the TV.

Soft heat warmed her skin, the brilliance making every cell of her glow. Then in a flash – a literal spark of lightning – she was on the other side. Heart pounding, breath coming in short, sharp gasps, it felt like a full-on panic attack was about to kick off. But what she saw stunned the nerves right out of her.

Amber gazed around in jaw-dropped amazement. She was at the top of a sprawling skyscraper, in a vast room made almost completely of crystal-clear glass. Like being outside yet inside.

Rays of sunlight refracted in rainbowed radiance. Fluffy, billowing clouds hung like puffs of peach candyfloss just beyond the invisible walls. They floated in purplish-blue skies, almost close enough to be touched.

Below was a city of tall, silver buildings with diamond spires. A gushing river of liquid sapphire zigzagged beside the buildings, with countless curving bridges dotted along its incredible length. It was at once mystical and futuristic, and the most wonderful thing Amber had ever seen.

'Welcome to Evadne!' Randall declared, suddenly materialising next to her. 'The birthplace of all fairy tales.'

'This … this is … *brilliant*!' Amber finally gasped.

'It really is something, isn't it?' Randall smiled, staring out at the view.

Giving a short growl at his crew, Wolf excused himself. 'Aye, while you two admire the scenery, I'll get the cubs onto their scooters and send them off back to the Warehouse.' He herded his brood out of the room towards the lift.

Randall turned to the view once more. 'I never grow tired of admiring it. Year upon year, I've been coming to Evadne. It's more home than any place else, really.' He turned to Amber in earnest. 'I'm happy to be sharing it with someone who's long been due a shot of wonder!'

Amber smiled. 'It's amazing.' She did a little twirl, her eyes darting everywhere. She took in the sprawling space, top to bottom with unfamiliar gadgets and trinkets. Just like the city beneath them – a mesh of the modern and the mythical, magic and science working together.

'I was going to ease you into everything,' Randall started. 'That was the plan. But now that's gone out the window. So, here we go.' Reaching his hand into his shirt pocket – the very same gesture she'd found so irritating not so long before – her uncle brought out a gold-laminated business card. He smiled, handing it to Amber.

On the front of the card, printed in whirling silver letters, Amber saw the words:

Presto! Magical Recovery Co.

Her brow furrowed. 'What is this? What does it mean?'

Randall beamed. 'It means there's so much more to life, Amber, dear. There's so much more to *everything*.'

Amber was starting to think that this was an understatement.

'Through quantum physics, it's possible to access different worlds within our world,' he went on to explain. 'These are called the Hidden Realms, which are known to only a few humans from our world. And this is my workshop, where I spend most days.'

'But … I thought you were a professor of Physics?' Amber asked.

'I am, child, I am. But my job is very different from most professors. If anyone in the Realms needs anything recovered, Presto! is where they come. I haven't failed at a case yet!' Randall paused for a moment and frowned. 'We are shaking it up a bit though, with Red. Finding a whole missing person is certainly trickier. But at Presto! we're nothing if not up for a challenge! Sure, our numbers have dwindled since we started – actually it's just been me for the longest while – but now *you're* here!'

Amber tried to imagine what sort of clientele stepped into Presto! on an average day. Did giants squeeze through the door, stomping across the floor and complaining that little boys had been stealing their gold? Or a wicked fairy asking for help to find where she'd left her spinning wheel?

'Please don't tell me you two are still just standing around chin wagging,' growled Wolf, striding into the room. 'We don't have a moment to lose!'

Randall perched himself on a chair, which had no legs or wheels. Only a bright shaft of light from the floor held it up.

'You hanging in there okay?' he asked Amber, who just about managed a dazed nod in return. Randall winked and gave a thumbs up, before expertly swinging around in the chair and turning on the high-tech gadgetry in front of him. At each flick of a switch, wide pixelated displays sprang up around them as monitors beeped and flashed on.

'Your screen, please, Wolf.' Randall held out an open palm. Wolf handed over the tablet. 'Thank you, kind sir!' said Randall.

Amber was surprised to see her uncle toss the block up into the air, and even more surprised when it was caught by a beam of light from one of the screens and immediately stretched open. She could just imagine Mr Maguire's face if he laid eyes on these monitors. It would blow his mind. She itched to ask endless questions about the tech, but she had the feeling that Wolf might rediscover his 'Big Bad' side if she delayed things any further. Although he claimed to be reformed, he still looked just as scary as he was hairy.

Randall flicked yet more switches. The scattered screens came swiftly together, merging into one huge display. 'Now, let's see if we can boost the signal from Red's tracker,' he said.

There was more switch-flicking and button-pushing. Then, finally, a loud high-pitched *ping* and a soft red dot flashed up on the edge of the screen.

'Yes!' Wolf exclaimed. 'You've got him, Prof! You've found the rascally wain!'

Randall seemed less excited. 'Hmm. Not all good news, I'm afraid.' Spreading his fingers across the screen, he expanded the red dot, bringing up an aerial map. 'The signal seems to be coming from the worst part of the Wizen Plains.'

Amber leaned in for a closer look. 'The what now?'

Wolf growled, his facial fur twitching.

I'm guessing not something good, Amber thought, not daring to say it out loud.

Randall adjusted his spectacles and scrolled further to bring up a visual. 'Feast your eyes on the Wizen Plains.'

If Evadne was sparkling brilliance, the place on the screen in front of them was the exact opposite. Dark, desolate and wind-battered, it looked as though it had never seen a glimmer of sunlight.

As the dot on the screen gave one last *ping* before disappearing altogether, Wolf let out a distraught growl. 'What just happened? No, no, no! Where's the signal gone? Get it back up, Prof. We need that intel!'

'No can do,' Randall said. 'The signal was very weak to begin with. Not even my ultra-modded detectors can restore it. We'll just have to make the most of the information we've got so far.' He expanded the screen with another flick. 'From what I can tell, Red is lost somewhere in the Wicked Witch's territory. If we have any hope of finding him, we're going to need the help of the only kids to ever make it out of there alive.'

Amber looked curiously from her uncle to Wolf.

'Hans and G,' Wolf said.

'Or, as they're commonly known,' Randall said, turning to Amber, 'Hansel and Gretel.'

'As in, the gingerbread house and trail of breadcrumbs?' Amber's eyes nearly popped out of her head.

Life with her uncle was just getting weirder and weirder!

Chapter Eight

HANS AND G

At that moment, Hans and G were in a race to see who could get to the kitchen first. They moved in unison, matching each other stride for stride, competitiveness in every step. With impressive agility and speed, they bulleted past the rows of framed photographs that lined the walls. Snapshot after snapshot showed the two of them holding up gold-plated trophies or with gold medals piled high around their necks. A shiny sequence of awards and plaques from the many martial arts competitions, where they always came in first place, sat in a trophy cabinet. Certified tenth-degree black belts, the twins were an undefeatable team.

They even looked alike. Both had their father's straight, jet-black hair, cut in a similar style. G liked to keep hers short, unobtrusive – very much like her brother's. They dressed the same too: a pair of close-fitting cargo trousers, long-sleeved polo-neck shirts and light sandals, all in black. The only major difference between them was their eyes. While Hans had his father's deep-set black eyes, G had inherited her mother's almond-shaped hazel gaze.

As they skidded to a halt in the kitchen, the woman bending over a hot oven straightened and faced them with a smile. Hans and G grinned back. Rosina had brought a comforting softness into their lives. Of course, they would always miss their mother, their dearest okāsan, who'd passed away when they were only little. But when Rosina married their father, she turned out to be the best bonus mother any kids could ask for.

'Hey there! Just in time for dinner.' The sunlight caught Rosina's golden curls, which were every bit as bouncy as her personality. She set down a roast chicken in the middle of a neatly-laid dinner table.

Hans and G sat down, instantly ravenous. At that moment, their father walked through the door.

'Hello! Hello!' he greeted cheerfully, taking off his sheriff's hat and striding over to kiss Rosina's rosy cheek and the tops of the twins' heads.

As the main protector of The Evergreen, Woodcutter Kayne often had to work long hours at the Forestry Department. In these parts, the Department not only cared for the woods but also enforced the rule of law. As sheriff, Woodcutter Kayne had his work cut out for him, but he always made a point of being home for dinner.

He carefully unslung his axe from across his back, placing it in a self-locking shelf cupboard by the door. A petrifying weapon with actual paralytic powers, it had to be handled with care and definitely could not be left lying around.

'How's everything?' He sat down at the head of the table. 'School okay?'

'Great!' Hans and G said together, as was often the case. It was a twin thing.

Floral dress flapping lightly as she moved, Rosina dished up the food and hummed a soft tune. 'Oh, and I have something extra special baked for after!' she cooed. 'A new recipe I'm trying out.'

Hans and G were keen on that. Rosina was an amazing cook. Especially when it came to baking. She made spectacular cakes and treats for the family every single day.

'Training session tonight, remember,' Woodcutter Kayne told the twins.

As if they would ever forget. If Hans and G weren't at school or busy with schoolwork, they were training. It was a schedule they'd been rigorously following for years. Their father, a martial arts black belt, had taken on the role of coach. Every other night, he led a practice session in the forest.

The rest of the time, Hans and G made sure to train on their own.

It was important for them to be physically fit and able to protect themselves – something that proved well worth the effort during a certain incident in the Wizen Plains some four years gone, when a certain Wicked Witch had caused a cauldron-full of trouble and trapped them in a cage. It was thanks to their training that they had managed to escape.

'Anything planned while we're out, my love?' Woodcutter Kayne asked Rosina, tucking into a large mouthful of shepherd's pie.

'I might pop round the knitting club,' Rosina replied. 'I haven't been in an age.'

'Oh, I thought you went just the other day?'

'No, not the knitting club. That was the embroidery class.'

'Ah, that's right. You're always so busy, it's no wonder I get mixed up.'

Rosina laughed merrily. 'I like to keep myself occupied!'

When the meal was done, Rosina sweetly waved

from the window, as Woodcutter Kayne led the way through the thicket towards Hans and G's favourite training spot. It was a particularly wide clearing near the edge of The Evergreen. He set a brisk pace, but the twins didn't even break a sweat. They were used to their father pushing them to their limits. In fact, they thrived on it.

As far as they were concerned, there was no one in all the Realms who would ever be able to beat them.

Chapter Nine

THE EVERGREEN

Randall spun round in his floating chair one more time. 'First port of call: The Evergreen!' he announced, powering down the gadgets around them.

Amber tried to keep up, head turning to follow him across the room. 'Dare I ask what that is?'

'Oh, only the most magical place you've ever seen,' her uncle replied, moving to stand in front of a tall object covered by an opaque sheet.

I can't imagine anywhere more magical than this, Amber thought, about to be proved very wrong indeed.

'Who's ready to travel by reflection?' With a dramatic swish, Randall pulled down the sheet to reveal a ten-foot mirror edged with gold. It was long and wide, capturing the group's full reflection. 'This is the most effective mode of transportation in these parts.'

Amber's eyes ran across the full width of the mirror. 'You mean you can travel to anywhere using this mirror?' she asked, a bolt of excitement shooting through her.

'Well, anywhere within the Hidden Realms,' Randall said. He rolled up a sleeve to reveal his snazzy cyber watch. 'Not only does this have excellent communication capabilities, as our dear friend Wolf here demonstrated earlier with his bazillion missed calls—'

Wolf grunted and Amber couldn't help but giggle.

'I've also fitted it with a Teleportation Element that allows for travel from one reflective surface to another. Shall we?' He pushed a side button on the watch. Instantly, the mirror turned gooey and bright, like it was melting. Tiny ripples and waves appeared where the glass had once been. 'Onwards!' Randall declared.

One by one, they stepped through the mirror.

Amber was surprised to find herself in water. For a moment, a familiar anxiety gripped her, and she struggled to catch her breath, expecting to choke – until she realised that not only could she not feel the water, but she was also bone-dry. Gaping in astonishment, she followed her uncle and Wolf onto the banks of what seemed to be a lake. She gazed around in total awe for the second time that day. Amber supposed she should be getting used to this sense of wonder, but she couldn't imagine that she ever would.

Randall had not been joking. The Evergreen was a phenomenal place, brimming with vibrant greenery. Amber could see lush forests with trees of all shapes and sizes. Bristling shrubberies and fluttering flowers of deep velvets, dazzling oranges, shimmering emeralds, sparkly whites and all the other colours of the rainbow.

It was as though Amber had stepped into an absolute paradise. Even if she could have captured a snapshot of it, she was sure nobody would ever believe that it really existed. Her ex-friend Katie would be in selfie heaven if she were here. But Katie was far away, back in the world Amber had left behind.

She breathed in deeply. The scent of the crisp, fresh air filled her nostrils, mingled with a delicious tinge of pine and vegetation sweetness.

'Well, well, well. If it isn't the old criminal himself.'

Amber shielded her eyes from the dazzle of a golden sun to see a bulky man in uniform with two identical children close behind him. The man was looking directly at Wolf.

'Woodcutter Kayne,' Wolf said gruffly.

If Amber didn't know better, she would've sworn that Wolf had gone pale beneath his fur.

'Keeping out of trouble, are we?' The Woodcutter was brusque, and he gave off a strong no-nonsense vibe. He was clearly not someone Amber would want to get on the wrong side of. And from the way the usually fearless creature was currently shifting nervously from paw to paw, it was pretty obvious that Wolf was thinking exactly same thing.

'Aye!' he exclaimed. 'Always out of trouble now.'

'Still shapeshifting?'

Wh– Whhattt? Amber blinked. *Wolf has shapeshifting abilities?* Would she ever stop being surprised? Somehow, in this new world, she didn't think so.

Wolf let out a laugh that sounded distinctly anxious. 'Have no reason to shapeshift these days. That life of crime is well and truly behind me!'

'I would hope so,' said the Woodcutter. 'The axe is always on standby. If you ever try to hurt Gran Red, you'll have me to answer to. You've had a taste

83

of the ol' chop once. Wouldn't want a repeat of it, now, would we?'

Amber suddenly realised that he was referring to the Little Red Riding Hood fairy tale.

No wonder Wolf is scared of Woodcutter Kayne! The Woodcutter in that story was almost the end of him.

'Nope, definitely not! Legitimate business owner here,' Wolf said quickly. 'Anyway, fancy running into you like this, Sheriff! Proper timing or what? We were just on our way to your house.'

At this point, Randall stepped forwards and the two men shook hands.

'Professor Abeiro! I didn't notice you there,' said the Woodcutter. 'We've met before. When Hans and G lost their way in the Wizen Plains, you deployed drones to help in the search.'

'Brilliant to see you again, Sheriff Kayne.' Randall smiled. 'And Hans and G! My goodness, how you two have sprouted!' He pushed Amber towards the twins. 'These are the famed pair who managed to defeat a very nasty witch indeed, my dear.'

Amber looked curiously at the boy and girl in front of her. They were nothing like she'd imagined when she'd read the fairy tale as a young child.

But hang on! Is the Woodcutter in Little Red Riding Hood the same one as in the Hansel and Gretel story? Amber's head was beginning to hurt.

'Escaped from that little cage and shoved the Wicked Witch right into the oven,' Hans said, proudly.

'Lucky for her it wasn't turned on just then,' G chimed in.

Amber couldn't imagine these two as helpless kids lost in the woods. Brimming with confidence, they didn't look like the types to be lured into a trap by anyone.

G carried on speaking, feisty and confident. 'The old hag ended up with a nasty banged head. Gave us plenty of time to get away.'

'By the time she came around, we were long gone,' added Hans.

'Still owe her a proper challenge, though.'

'Yeah. She won't be so lucky next time.'

Randall clapped his hands together, smiling. 'And that is the exact reason we are here. We need you to help us rescue Red from her clutches.'

The twins looked at each other with devilish grins. 'We're in!' they said as one.

Chapter Ten

TRAPPED

Shuffling into an upright sitting position, Red brought a soot-covered hand to his pounding head, making his hair just as ashy as the rest of him. *Oh, great.* It was an effort to get his spiky platinum locks to look just right – the amount of hair gel alone!

Every part of him hurt. The hectic fall from his bike, the abduction by the crazy witch – all of it had left him thoroughly bruised and battered. As the memories of how he'd got into this sticky situation flooded back into his mind, he had a pang of fear for his bike. Was it lying mangled in the middle of Wizen nowhere? How in the cosmos would he get it back? He couldn't be Racer Red without his star bike! And judging by the tattered state of his hood, he would also have to throw that away for sure. Red Riding Hood with no bike and no hood? A tragedy for the ages.

Eyes open a crack, vision blurry, he tried to look around and find out exactly where he'd ended up. At that moment, he understood why his head was slamming: his de-leviters were gone. His specialised goggles were the only thing that controlled the light sensitivity of his eyes. Without them, the faintest glow seemed excessively bright and neon-coloured spots distorted his vision. It was a combination that brought on a brain-splitting headache that no one except Red could possibly imagine.

Red tried to focus through the throbbing in his head. Slowly and painfully, he managed to drag himself to his feet by grabbing onto what felt like metal bars behind him. Yes, they were definitely bars. From the little he could see; he was trapped in some sort of cage.

Head thumping, eardrums banging, Red took a painful step forward. It was like trying to walk on water. (The sensitivity to light badly affected his balance too.) Everything around him spun, and right then, keeping upright seemed almost impossible. When he finally got to the other side of the cage, Red was exhausted.

Maybe he shouldn't have been such a hot head with his gran after all. If he hadn't fobbed off Keeper Academy in favour of working with the Loopy Looters, he wouldn't be in this mess. Then again, the whole 'training to be the future Keeper of the Cosmos' thing was more pressure than a thirteen-year-old boy needed. It might be family tradition, but what if he had other plans? What if he wanted other things from life?

Nope. No regrets. Blowing off Keeper Academy for another year had been the right decision. He would get out of this cage somehow – preferably with a little style and flair.

Red crawled from end to end of the cage and discovered that the dastardly thing was suspended from the ceiling, about two metres from the ground. Maybe if he got it to swing, the cage would hit the nearest wall and break.

Trying to ignore his migraine and dizziness, Red got to work. Running end to end, he gathered momentum. The cage started to swing. One swing. Two. Three ... Six ... Ten ... And finally, success! The cage slammed into the back wall, smashing completely open.

Yes! Red tumbled to the ground. If he'd been sore before, he was in agony now. But what was pain compared with freedom?

Feeling around the cold stone floor, he set about searching for his de-leviters. Without them, he wouldn't get very far at all.

A few fumbles led him to a tabletop of rubbish. Another stroke of luck! In the midst of what felt like old trinkets, broken figurines and tattered plush toys were his precious goggles, tucked between dusty crystals and dried fruit. Triumphantly, Red pulled them out and put them on. Immediately, the splitting headache ebbed away, and his vision returned to normal. He was ready to escape.

But as he geared up for the run of his life, he suddenly realised that there was no place to run to – or rather, run *through*. Looking around at steaming cauldron pots, the burning hot oven, dusty, drab furniture and more junk than a junkyard, he found that there wasn't a door or window in sight. Just a wide, completely enclosed cavern.

'Red, darling, you didn't think it'd be that easy, did you?'

Red spun around.

The Wicked Witch lounged lazily on a stone throne, laughing. She'd appeared from thin air. 'I learned my lesson long ago about little children and cages, thanks to Hansel and Gretel,' she hissed. 'I'm not making the same mistake twice!'

She summoned a blast of icy wind and blew Red back into the magically reconstructed cage.

'You're my very special guest,' she told him. 'Finally, after years of languishing in the dark, decades of oppression and deprivation, my time in the limelight has come,' she cackled, pacing up and down almost giddily. 'No more horrid underground bunkers for me, no more hiding and scurrying like a rat. Unmatched glory is within my reach. And you, my puny captive, are the key. You're going to get me your gran's secret codes.'

Red's brow furrowed. 'What do you mean?'

'You see, dear prisoner,' she said with a smirk, 'there are fragments of a magic-infused Spindle Whorl scattered across the Realms. These individual pieces are made of star power. If someone was to put the Spindle Whorl together again, it would be the most powerful weapon in all the universe. Your gran's codes are the only way to do it. And *you*, dearest Red, are going to help me get them!'

Chapter Eleven

DETOUR

Amber stood in Hans and G's home, examining the framed photographs that the twins had raced past earlier. Their accomplishments were displayed with pride. Amber thought of the minimalistic pristine walls of her own home and frowned.

'We're competitive.' A voice behind her made Amber jump. 'Can you tell?' It was G.

Amber smiled. 'Just a little. So how many tournaments have you won?'

'Oh, loads.' There was no bragging to it, just a statement of fact. 'We try to enter one each week if we can. Keeps us on our toes.'

'You must be really good.'

G laughed. 'We try.'

Amber's eyes continued to run across the length of the display before coming to a stop at a family portrait. She pointed to a beautiful blonde woman positioned between Woodcutter Kayne and the twins. 'Who is that?'

'Rosina,' G said. 'She married Father and adopted us, too. She's the best.' There was warmth and admiration in her tone.

'But I thought your stepmother was evil?' Amber said, thinking about the second wife in the fairy tale she knew practically by heart.

'Not Rosina,' said G. 'You shouldn't believe everything you read.'

Just then a call came from the kitchen. 'Girls!'

G grinned. 'We're being summoned. Come on!'

She grabbed Amber's hand and pulled her along behind her.

Randall was at the kitchen table, Wolf and Hans on either side of him. Woodcutter Kayne was leaning on his axe.

'Bit of a bump in the road,' said Randall, as the girls pulled out chairs and sat down. 'Unfortunately, the Teleportation Element is glitching out. Some connecting cells are fizzling a little. The replacements are back at the London office. We need to go back for them. Wouldn't want to be trapped in these Realms forever!'

Trapped? Amber thought. Although Evadne and The Evergreen were amazing, eternity in fairy tale lands was not something she'd bargained for. Her parents might drive her around the bend, but she couldn't imagine never seeing them again.

'Ready when you are,' she said quickly. 'When do we leave?'

Randall was already on his feet. 'Straight away. Hans, G, if you could come along too. We can go straight for Red after.'

'Sure!' Hans and G answered as one.

'Don't forget me,' Wolf growled. 'Red's my responsibility. If we can figure out how to get him back, I'm all for it.'

'Right,' Randall said. 'Onwards then.'

Woodcutter Kayne turned to the twins. 'I know you two are more than capable of handling yourselves, but if at any point you need anything,' he gestured to the wristbands the three of them wore, 'hit the red and I'll be there quicker than you can say "trail of breadcrumbs", okay?'

The twins nodded. Their father ruffled their hair affectionately. 'I must get back to work. The forest needs me. Good luck with your quest, Professor Abeiro. And take good care of my kids.'

'You have my word, Sheriff,' said Randall.

Amber, Hans, G, Wolf and Randall were huddled together in her uncle's living room in Brixton. Looking at a clock on the wall, Amber blinked in shock. No time had passed from the moment she and Randall had left till now. The quantum leaping seemed to adhere to its own timescale and didn't seem to align with Earth's time at all.

Randall set the element cell-merger on the coffee table in the middle of the room. He detached something from the back of his cyber watch and placed it on an aluminium stand inside the cell-merger. He shut the little door on the outside and a soft hum began to emit from it.

'What's that sound?' Amber asked, as Wolf paced up and down impatiently.

'That's the charging mechanism kicking into gear,' her uncle replied, setting a remote control on the coffee table. 'The watch is powered by Angelpyrite, but it has to be fully charged to work. Shouldn't be more than a few minutes,' Randall said. 'As soon as that's done, we can begin—'

A loud rapping on the front door cut him off.

'Who in heavens could that be?' As Randall went to get the door, the rest of the group shuffled as far into the background as possible to avoid detection.

97

Wolf, Hans and G stepped into the adjoining office, while Amber tried to lean casually against one wall in the hallway. Although she seemed to have completely forgotten where to place her arms or legs.

Randall pulled the door open by the tiniest fraction. Through the crack, Amber could see a boy with large, face-engulfing glasses, neatly trimmed Afro hair, dressed like a businessman about to head off for a spot of golfing. Polo shirt, plaid vest and well-pressed khaki trousers.

'Good evening, Professor Abeiro,' the boy began, in an arrogant, snooty sort of voice. 'Might I have a word?'

'Well, hi there, Bobby,' Randall greeted him. 'What's up?'

'What is "up", Professor, is that you are making somewhat of a racket up here. And for those of us who live directly beneath you – like my family and I – it is a terrible inconvenience.'

'Ah. I see. Your mother is asking us to keep it down?' Randall guessed.

'Mostly me, sir.'

'Right. I hear you, Bobby. We will keep it down.'

'I think you must have visitors?' The boy went on, trying to peer behind Randall. 'I thought I saw a girl with suitcases earlier.'

Randall gestured to Amber behind him but didn't fully open the door. 'That would be my niece. Now, young man, are the investigations at an end? We're just in the middle of something.'

'You know what, if I didn't know better, I would think you might be involved in something suspicious, Professor.'

This nosey neighbour doesn't know when to stop, thought Amber.

'But of course you do know better,' Randall said. 'Now, please excuse us, Bobby. Let your mother know we'll keep it down.'

Before the boy could say anything else, Randall shut the door.

Chapter Twelve

DANGEROUS DALLIANCES

Bobby bristled with annoyance. Who in the bejeebers did that quack of a professor think he was? The man was always banging around, up to goodness knows what. Then he had the audacity to slam a door in Bobby's face. *Rude!*

Well, if he thought he could just brush off Bobby J. Kingston and carry on with that racket, he had another think coming. Bobby had had enough. Tonight, he would finally get to the bottom of what exactly went on in Apartment 1A.

Still fuming, Bobby thundered down the stairs back to his family's flat. Slamming the front door behind him, he ignored his mother's questions about where he'd been. She and his nan were watching some soap opera. His baby brother cooed on a mat, surrounded by soft toys.

I'm doing this for them, Bobby told himself. It was always weird noises with that man upstairs. Furniture constantly scraping across floorboards, odd banging sounds and even thudding of boots – as though there were untold multitudes trekking in and out the place! What if the shenanigans he had going on up there were to spill over and affect them down here? What then? Well, as the man of the house, Bobby wouldn't let anything cuckoo bananas happen on his watch.

Stomping into his bedroom, he immediately

made for the window by his bedside and opened it wide. The warm evening air felt pleasant on his face. Bobby frowned. He could see the bottom of Randall Abeiro's balcony. Now, if he could just get up there – if he could get *onto* the balcony, he would finally be able to see what went on in that place.

What to use? What to use? Aha!

Bobby eyed the drainpipe to the side of the window – that could take his weight. Wouldn't be too hard to scale up to the professor's flat. Bobby wasn't the biggest of guys, but he was definitely strong.

Without further delay, he climbed out of the window and carefully positioned himself so he could grasp the drainpipe. Then he clambered up, slow and steady. With luck on his side, he managed to reach his goal without incident and soon found himself standing firmly on Randall's balcony. Inching to the edge, so as not to be spotted by those inside, he craned his neck to peep through the partially open curtain in front of the glass door. Heart thumping, excitement pulsing through him, he grinned in anticipation of what he would see;

the surprising exposé. Yet a quick scan of the living room revealed ... nothing.

Bobby huffed in disappointment. Empty. And from what he could tell, the other rooms were unoccupied too.

He couldn't understand where they'd got to. Had they left the building? *No. Impossible.* It was less than five minutes since he'd had the door so rudely shut in his face. He would have seen them coming out onto the pavement below.

So, if they weren't in the apartment and they hadn't left the building, where on earth were they? Weirdly, they'd left their TV on ...

Meanwhile, Amber, Hans, G, Randall and Wolf were back in the workshop in Evadne.

'Would it be so bad to just storm the place and grab Red?' Hans asked.

Randall shook his head. 'It's unwise to try and confront the Wicked Witch directly. With her use of the dark arts, we would have a very difficult challenge on our hands. Not to mention her high levels of manipulation and trickery.' He began to pace. 'No, if we are to do this, it has to be through stealth. Which happens to be something of a breeze for someone like me. I have a couple of tricks of my own!'

As Randall fiddled with some controls, Amber gasped as a full-on hologram appeared in the middle of the room. It grew and grew until it filled half the length of the workshop floor and stretched right up to the ceiling.

'Welcome to the Wicked Witch's lair,' declared Randall.

From the outside, it looked like a normal sand dune. The only difference were the reflective panels along its width.

'The panels capture light from the seven red moons of the Wizen Plains. It powers her whole base.' Randall pointed with a customised luminous stick. 'They also serve as the Witch's surveillance system. And if you look through a simulation X-ray lens ...' He pushed another button on the controls.

Dust and earth filtered away to reveal what lay within the dune. Inside was a deep and spacious cavern with jagged stone steps built into the back. The steps led up to a hatch at the top of the upper interior surface.

G moved closer to where the image of the hatch shimmered. 'That was how the Wicked Witch caught us,' she said.

Amber frowned. 'Hang on, I thought you were lured in by a gingerbread house,' she said.

Hans snorted. 'I wish.'

Amber blinked. Randall had been right: no one could imagine the full scope of how things *really* were in fairy tale lands. All the stories she had been told when she was small were just the tip of it all.

'It's definitely a trap,' Randall said. He magnified the hatch on the hologram. 'The indication here is that the hatch is rarely opened. It's crusted over with dirt, which looks to have accumulated over the years. It's also sealed with titanium bolts. Not an issue for the Wicked Witch herself, of course; she teleports everywhere.'

'She uses chemicals,' G said. 'Mixes them in a cauldron and pours them into little glass globes. All she has to do is smash 'em on the ground and she disappears in a cloud of smoke.'

'That sounds about right.' Randall touched a hand to the side of his spectacles. 'Hmm, that bolted hatch poses a problem. It's the only entrance or exit point for the cavern and recovering Red.'

'What about the Teleportation Element?' Amber asked, determined to be useful. 'Couldn't we use that to teleport ourselves in and out of the lair?'

'I wish that were possible, my dear. But the Wicked Witch uses a protective forcefield to insulate the walls of her hideout. It's a kind of firewall that blocks any electronic or atomical impulses of interference. The Teleportation Element would be useless, I'm afraid.' He paused. 'No. What would give us the best hope of reaching our friend Red would be to lure Ms Witch out of and away from her lair. At that point we could then disable the firewall, before breaking through the hatch. Good old-fashioned infiltration and extraction of magical valuables!'

Amber tried to nod wisely, but to be honest, she had understood about one word in ten that her uncle had just said. She just wished she could help.

'The Woodcutter could be of use,' Wolf suggested. 'He could cause some commotion close to the Wicked Witch's lair? Keep the foul lassie busy with that, while we—'

'Infiltrate the lair!' Randall finished Wolf's thought for him. 'Not a shabby idea there, Wolf. Not shabby at all. From there, we could have our young tech whizz bring down the firewall.'

He looked straight at Amber.

'Me?' she gasped. A few seconds earlier, she had wished she could help. But now it actually seemed like she might be able to, the familiar doubts started creeping in. Anxiety prickled at the back of her neck.

'Amber-Ramber, you don't give yourself enough credit,' Randall said, as if he knew exactly what she was thinking. 'Your father has told me about the codes you've built for friends, classmates, even teachers; the gadgets and technologies you've created in your room. He says they're phenomenal.'

Amber blinked in confusion. Her father had never said anything to her about coding, other than it being a distraction from her schoolwork. Had he really told Randall that her work was phenomenal? And when exactly were all these secret conversations happening? She didn't think her father and Randall spoke!

'Your dad is prouder of you than you know,' Randall continued. 'He has other reasons for not being so keen on technology. But if anyone can do this, you can.'

As Amber took in his words, some of the jitters ebbed away.

'When all this is over, I promise I'll tell you more about my relationship with your dad. But right now, we have to focus. I'll give you plenty of coaching beforehand – the ins and outs of the whole system,' Randall assured her. 'This isn't your average firewall. We're talking about the Wicked Witch here.'

'Don't we know it!' Hans and G said at the same time.

Laughter filled the room, easing some of the tension.

'Which brings us to you two,' Randall turned to the twins. 'Once the forcefield is down, you will need those famous martial arts skills to get to the hatch without being seen. At that point ...' He reached into a cupboard behind him, rummaging for a second or two before returning with an oval metal object. It fitted easily in the palm of his hand. 'This is an unlocking trijector. It has a morphing encryption that imbeds itself into the shaft of any lock, forcing it open. It can also work out the code of any keypad in seconds. It will unseal the titanium bolts. Lastly, our friend Wolf here will come into the mix.' He turned to Wolf. 'Do you think your brawn can handle lifting the hatch?'

Wolf raised his massive arms and flexed his bulging muscles, eyes glinting. 'Can a hound howl?'

Randall grinned. 'That will be that, then. The only thing left will be for me to get in there and steal Red away. My most ambitious heist yet!'

Chapter Thirteen

GLITCHES
IN THE COSMOS

Galactica Eireen. The nickname Gran Red had gotten in school had stuck. It wasn't just the fact that she was heiress to Evadne's Consortia of Keepers that earned her the title. That wasn't much of a big deal at Keeper Academy: all the kids there were bloodline to the Consortia of Keepers. No, what had set Eireen apart had been her exceptional skill at galactic weaving. A real talent, each one of her teachers had agreed. The job of any Keeper of the Cosmos – what every single pupil at Keeper Academy was training for – involved charting stars across multiple universes using distinct celestial cartography: telescopic projections, star maps and a collection of other astronomical equipment. Top of her class, year after year, Eireen had been a whizz at this. And so the fame of Galactica Eireen grew.

That was who she had been known as for the majority of her earlier years. But now, in the winter of her life, old age firmly knocking at her door, she had earned a new nickname: Gran Red. She was grandmother to the famed street racer Red Riding Hood – of whom she could not be prouder if she tried. Of course, they did not always see eye to eye, especially when it came to the family business. And it was true, the lad had an alarming recklessness about him, but he was a good kid. He was also good to her – that is, whenever she could get hold of him.

She mostly never knew where the boy was these days, since he'd started working with Wolf and the Loopy Looters. He'd become even harder to pin down than ever. Racer Red whom no one could ever catch. Even his gran.

Despite the name change, Gran Red carried on, doing what she'd always done best: charting the stars.

She had always happily carried out this duty in the Glass Cottage in the valley of The Evergreen. Over the centuries, the cottage had become an extension of the valley around it; the succulent shrubbery now grew inside as well, carpeting every floor, and each room teamed with life. Only at the ceiling did the greenery end, and a twinkling starlit sky began, a dancing, spiralling, bending of light that showed many hundreds of grouped stars.

On her charter's rocking chair, Gran Red was able to rise to the ceiling. It was like being in space. And these stars had much to tell. In their shifting patterns, Gran Red could see all life. Her one assignment was to monitor each of them, using Keeper codes linked to the astronomical equipment to maintain order in the Cosmos – the Cosmos made from all the Realms and beyond. Keeping it safe was the Consortia of Keepers' main task. They made sure that the powers of the stars stayed safe in a protective shield made of codes kept by generations of Keepers over the centuries. Keepers were taught from an early age how to create, control and update these codes. They could then use them to make shields that protected the stars and kept order in the Cosmos.

Now, looking deep into the skies spread before her, Gran Red could see strange patterns of sparks and flashes.

All was not as it should be.

Gran Red rose higher in her rocking chair, adjusting the view of her observational spectacles so she could take a closer look.

In all her years of charting the stars, she'd rarely seen this type of activity. Most alarming of all was where it was happening – in the Wicked Witch's territory. Could the Wicked Witch of the Wizen Plains be up to her old tricks again?

For many more decades than she cared to remember, it had been a large part of Gran Red's job to thwart the continual ploys of the Wicked Witch. Their pasts had been so tightly linked that there were times when Gran Red thought that their destinies must be intertwined too. Theirs was a history that stretched far back to Gran Red's academy days, when they were schoolgirls together.

Of course, back then, the Witch hadn't fully grown into her wickedness yet. In those days, she was just Nina and Gran Red was still Eireen.

Once upon a time, a baby girl of no known parentage had been abandoned at Keeper Academy … That was just one of the many rumours that the students whispered to each other about Nina – the hard-faced beauty with hair like snow and eyes like fire. Eireen had heard them all.

A brilliant scholar, outstanding overall, Nina unnerved as much as she inspired. She was always surrounded by eager followers, yet she didn't have any *real* friends. Which was why the fast and true connection she struck up with Eireen was so special.

When Eireen started her first year, Nina was a few months ahead of her and had already become an integral part of the school. Painfully shy and withdrawn, Eireen shuffled through one of the many hallways one day, clutching a crocheted purse full of shamrock-stencilled beads that her parents had sent her. It was something to remind her of home and keep her occupied in her spare time at Keeper Academy. Eireen loved looping the beads into bracelets or necklaces. She'd been on her way to pop the beads into a bowl on her dormitory nightstand – the three-leaf clover pattern would glimmer nicely under lamplight – when she'd collided head-on with Nina.

The beads tipped from her purse, scattering across the corridor. Eireen felt an intense dread as one of them rolled over and touched the tip of Nina's pointy-toed boot. The rumours about the girl swirled in Eireen's head: about her short-fuse temper and high-handed princess ways. Eireen expected to be yelled at, cursed at, possibly even kicked. What she didn't expect was for the majestically tall Nina to quietly drop to her knees and begin picking up the scattered trinkets.

Trembling slightly, Eireen dropped to the ground too and started gathering. Together, they picked up the beads. When all were retrieved and set back safely in the purse, the girls stood. Nina faced Eireen squarely. 'Are you a leprechaun?' she asked.

A flustered Eireen looked down at herself, smoothing the embroidered green and gold tunic Mammy had made for her, before patting her orange mass of curly hair. She was at a loss for a response and ended up attempting a joke, but it was delivered awkwardly. 'Oh yes, I just adore cobbling shoes, leaving pots of gold at the end of rainbows, that sort of thing.'

Nina gave her a long hard stare ... before bursting into laughter. She had a loud but surprisingly tinkly laugh. Eireen started laughing too. And that was that.

From then on, the girls were inseparable. Nina

took it upon herself to be Eireen's guide and teacher. She calmed Eireen's anxieties, showing her the ins and outs of academy life, and teaching her what it took to be successful. She helped Eireen to perfect the skills of reading and directing the stars, and of the spell crafting that harnessed star power. In return, Eireen offered the type of support Nina never felt she truly had at the school. Of course, Nina was popular, with teachers and students alike fawning over her, but genuine connections hadn't been something she'd ever experienced. With her gentle manner and complete loyalty, Eireen was a *real* friend to Nina. Complementing one another perfectly, they grew to be the best of friends.

But even the best of relationships can crumble. And the year of their seventeenth birthdays changed everything.

A loud alert sounded, shattering Gran Red's trip down memory lane. Long gone was the dear friend she used to know. The strange activity continued to flare up across the skies, its trail blazing right down from the Wizen Plains towards ... The Evergreen!

An attack was coming their way.

Gran Red knew she needed to call for backup. But first she had to know where her grandson was. Quickly reaching for her tele-communicator, she tapped in Red's number. The call disconnected immediately. She hit redial, trying several more times. Each with the same result. Instant disconnection. Real worry crept in, and she frantically tried to reach him on his other devices.

Still nothing.

Running out of patience, she finally dialled Wolf. The call connected and rang with no answer. An agitated Gran Red shut down the tele-communicator.

Where in the Wizen world are they?!

Chapter Fourteen

FIREWALL

'From my calculations, disabling the Wicked Witch's firewall is a five-step process,' Randall told Amber, Hans and G – Wolf having been dispatched back to The Evergreen to let the Woodcutter know the plan. 'I've come up with a simulation of sorts to mimic the internal framework of this firewall. This will create a series of probable variables that show what you can expect, Amber. Before having to deal with the real thing.'

'What will I use, though?' Amber asked, worried. 'All my stuff is back at the flat.'

'I've got you.' Again, Randall went rummaging in the cupboard that, like the room, was made completely of glass. Amber was beginning to suspect it was a kind of Presto! compartment of all things flashy and high-tech. Her kind of cupboard!

'Ah, yes, here they are,' Randall said. 'You're going to need these.'

'Gloves?' Amber stared in disbelief at the elbow-length satin gloves her uncle was holding out towards her. 'How on earth are gloves going to help?'

'These are not just any old gloves, dear child. I like to think of them as the ultimate net surfers! Try them on.'

Amber slipped both gloves on, noticing each one had a sparkling blue crystal at the wrist. As she gently tapped one, a pixelated forcefield sprung up. It encompassed Amber, illuminating her with multi-coloured data, scribblings and symbols.

As Amber spun around in awe, the twins let out a unified, 'Wow!'

'With these gloves,' Randall continued, 'you're not only *operating* the cyber network, but you are also positioned precisely *within* it. You're pretty much part of the system.'

Amber reached out a hand to the virtual walls around her. Each touch of her fingers made a *ping*, shooting tingles up her arm and down her body. She'd become digital.

'Now, there are about five or so cyber critters that act as guards. Only after bypassing these will you be able to break through to the Wicked Witch's network's mainframe. You can fight them by encrypting codes – you know, the normal coding you do when building websites and such. In essence, you basically write the code as you go, working out which code works best to eliminate each critter. Make sense?'

'Totally.' Amber nodded. If only Mr Maguire could see her now.

'Good. Though I should give fair warning – you will need caution and vigilance at all times. The critters are small but vicious.'

'The Wicked Witch has a pet name for them too,' G added. 'Calls them her "critty critts".'

Hans flinched, clearly also remembering. 'Suppose we were lucky we never had to face them directly,' he said.

'Yeah, once we had managed to knock the old crone unconscious, we were able to deactivate the firewall using codes we'd seen her use.'

'I take it those codes have since been changed?' Amber asked.

'Oh, yeah!' G answered. 'A lot about the place has changed since we were prisoners there. Like the hatch. That wasn't bolted or nearly as weighty as it is now. Back then, as soon as her firewall was down, Hans and I easily lifted it and ran.

'Yeah,' Hans agreed. 'This right now – this is next-level stuff.'

'Right.' Randall gave Amber an encouraging smile. 'I'm going to run through several simulations that will mimic the kinds of cyber critters you might expect to encounter. All you have to do is play with the data to outsmart it. Easy for someone with your talent.'

Amber had never thought of her 'hobby' quite like that before. She stood up a little straighter.

Maybe, just maybe, she could pull this off.

Chapter Fifteen

INTO THE
BLACKNESS

Caught up in the simulation, Amber couldn't see anything; only Randall's voice through her earpieces anchored her. Sparks came at her from every direction. She tried to catch her breath, to not let the blackness suffocate her.

Another sharp, hot ping hit her; this time hard in the back. Her eyes were shut. She couldn't open them. *Wouldn't* open them. She was too afraid. Randall had been wrong. She wasn't the person for the job. She didn't have what it took.

Cowering back, she shrank away from the attacks. It was all over. The cyber critters would devour her. She had let everyone down.

'Amber,' her uncle spoke calmly. 'Listen to the sound of my voice. Your creativity is power. Open your eyes, Amber.'

Amber opened them and saw a critter coming at her.

Stringy tentacles with arcs of electricity shooting out from a belly made of jelly. It glowered at her; a blob caught in a furnace of its own creation. Spurts of flames spiralled out of the hole on its wobbly head. Fire-critter.

Close behind was a googly-eyed creature with sharp incisors poking out from its bottom lip. Red all over, it had a ribbed bone-hard shell that looped into a spiky tail at the end. Scorpio-critter.

Next was a short and stocky manatee type of thing. Blue and leathery, its wrinkled skin folded and bulged with every move. Manatee-critter.

Behind it shuffled a clawed, lanky-limbed critter. Translucent and misty, it stretched tall and thin, spindly like a spider. Mist-critter.

Amber knew exactly what she needed to do.

A volley of vapourised data quenched the fire-critter's furnace breath. A ripple of electronic shots brought down the scorpio-critter. Icy HTML links froze the manatee-critter in its tracks, and JavaScript smoke clogged up the mist-critter, dissolving it into nothing.

On and on it went. Exercise after exercise until Amber could predict every critter's next move and counter it without error.

When the simulation finally powered down, cheers erupted in the room. The twins and Randall were impressed.

'Excellently done, Amby!' Randall gave her a huge hug.

The twins jumped at her with high-fives. 'Wow!' they chorused.

'Brilliant!' G said.

'Absolutely stunning!' Hans enthused.

More hugs and high-fives went round, though it wasn't long before Randall whipped out his luminous stick once more. He pointed at the activator crystals on the gloves. 'Again!'

Amber was airborne, hurtling through the clouds in the Presto! glider, further and further away from Evadne with each turbo thruster blast. A digital map took up a large portion of the main viewport – a wide glass pane that doubled as a windshield. It detailed the many dips and spikes of the surrounding area, outlining the possible location of the Wicked Witch's lair. The map was based mainly on Hans and G's memory, and the hope was that it would narrow down the search.

This is so wild. Amber sucked in a breath and looked at the landscape below them. *I'm in an actual sky machine, travelling with literal fairy tale creatures to rescue another fairy tale creature.* The word unbelievable came to mind!

Up front in the flight deck, she caught sight of Woodcutter Kayne's skycraft in the Presto! glider's HUD mini-map. Thankfully, Wolf had managed to get him on board, and the two were now on their way to the planned drop-off.

Amber adjusted her headgear. A bell-shaped cap of stretchy fibres fitted closely to the contours of her head, flattening the front of her fluffy hair. She had an earpiece looped over one ear, with an accompanying microphone attached to it.

The skyline and atmosphere changed, from the perpetual daylight and brilliance of Evadne, to an unfamiliar gritty dimness. Amber didn't need to be told that they'd reached the dreadsome Wizen Plains. A burnt orange hue tinged the air thanks to the scattered moons overhead.

Randall's voice interrupted her thoughts. 'Here we go.'

He began to lower the Presto! glider, and Amber got a clearer view of the Wizen Plains. Made mostly of craggy charcoal mountains, it was as bleak as she'd imagined. A thoroughly horrid place. She shivered at the thought of being lost out there. When Hans and G said they'd been lucky, they weren't joking.

Finally, the glider came to a stop at the base of a mountain. Amber unbuckled herself from her seat and stepped out with the others. Outside, in the muggy air, she got an instant lungful of sulphuric fumes. They were pungent and sickly. She spluttered.

'You alright?' Randall asked.

Amber gave a small nod, clearing her throat. It was a very unpleasant atmospheric composition, but she could take it.

She brought down the visor attached to her headgear, her eyes watering from the stinging ash blown on the wind. The weather was truly awful: windy blasts fluctuating between humidity and freezing cold. Bombarded by such extremes, she was glad of the protective suit Randall had given her from his treasure-trove. The stories Hans and G had told her of skin-ripping diamond rain had made her eagerly shimmy into the form-fitting black bodysuit made of specialised neoprene – weatherproof and, most importantly, damage proof.

We'll be fine, she told herself. *Won't we?*

'Bonnie gear,' Wolf winked, jumping out of Woodcutter Kayne's skycraft and thudding onto the dusty ground. His everyday, all-weather kilt was prevented from flapping in the wind by a clan-crested buckle on the front. Of course, he didn't need any protective gear. Thick, hardy fur was more than good enough.

Amber smiled. 'Thanks! "Superhero chic", I believe it's called.'

Wolf laughed.

'Honestly, I'm just relieved to be wearing something that Mother hasn't bought me!' As her thick, curly locks blew every which way in the wind, peeking out from beneath the back of the bell-cap, and with booted feet planted firmly on the ground, Amber felt more herself than she ever had done before.

'Wait for our confirmation that we've located the lair,' Randall instructed Woodcutter Kayne.

Woodcutter Kayne gave a thumbs up. With a small salute, he manoeuvred his skycraft up and away to await further instructions.

Wolf turned to Amber. 'Yer ready for this, lass?'

Amber paused. Her life so far couldn't have been further from where she was now, stalking into a witch's lair in an interdimensional world.

'Let's go!' she said with confidence. She was done with playing it safe!

Chapter Sixteen

WITCHES' BREW

Red stared at the Wicked Witch in horror. The intergalactic codes from the Keeper of the Cosmos would be dynamite in her hands. *Cosmic* dynamite. Every bit of the Realms would bend to her will and she would have unmatched power. He slammed angry fists at the cage. 'I will *never* in a trillion years help you, you nasty hag!'

'You are funny!' The Wicked Witch laughed. 'I have ways of making you change your mind about that, pip-squeak.' She let her gaze trail to the burning oven. She rose from her throne and started walking menacingly towards it and Red drew back in horror.

'So, my lovely,' the Wicked Witch sidestepped the oven and lifted a tray of what looked and smelled very much like cakes. 'What tickles your fancy? We have rabid-raspberry or vanilla-vice? Freshly baked this morning. They'll melt in your mouth and melt your brain at the same time!'

On a gold-rimmed baking tray were swirl-patterned cupcakes topped with glittering icing, dusted over with a generous coating of sugar. Even Red had to admit they looked delicious. Pity about the whole destroying a person's brain thing.

Tray in hand, the Wicked Witch glided towards Red. She hummed a tune that managed to sound eerily soft, sweet and terrifying all at the same time. With a wave of her fingers, she loosened his shackles, and the cage began to lower.

Red flexed his shoulder. As soon as the cage

touched the floor, he would grab his chance to escape. If he could just ram hard enough into Her Witchiness, he was sure he would be able to shove her straight into the oven.

Just like Hansel and Gretel. How did the old tale go again?

Two unfortunate children, lost in the Wizen Plains,
Came across a bunker, promising to relieve their pains.
Beneath the sandy dune they went, hoping to lay,
Regain strength, maybe even play.
What happened next proved to be a nightmare,
All who hear this tale, take heed and beware.
The Wicked Witch, full of hate,
Had lured them there with clever bait.
Soon captive and cold, the children were thoroughly broke.
Until came a moment that gave some sliver of hope.
Into her own oven they shoved the vile vixen,

and made their escape into the Wizen.

They thought she was truly gone!

But, unhappily for the Cosmos and beyond,

the Wicked Witch survived fiery decay

to terrorise again another day.

Well, this time would be different. There would be no survival for the Wicked Witch. Red was finally going to finish the job the twins had started all those years ago.

As Red prepared to make his move, the Presto! team gathered just outside the Wicked Witch's lair. Crouching in the ash-dirt, they huddled behind an outcropping of large craggy boulders. With their bodies pressed tightly against the cold stones, they had a good view of where the bunker lay. Randall signalled Woodcutter Kayne.

While Red watched his cage door slide open, Woodcutter Kayne's skycraft whizzed out of hiding to slice through the air, destination co-ordinates entered and locked in. The Wicked Witch almost had a foot in the cage and Red's shoulders were hunched, ready for combat, when Woodcutter Kayne's skycraft hovered over the lair.

The intrusive whirring of the machine startled both the Wicked Witch and Red. Simultaneously, they looked up to where the noise was coming from. Then, a fraction of a second later, the Wicked Witch slammed the cage door shut.

'What in the cursed wretchedness …?' she shrieked.

Her frustration was obvious in her every move as she set down her precious cakes. With another swish, she had Red gagged and bound.

'No one interrupts me. *No one!*'

'Okay, this is it.' Woodcutter Kayne's voice rang out through the telecom apparatus. 'She's coming out. I repeat, the Wicked Witch is coming out.'

At that moment, a boiling black mass of cloud rose from the Wicked Witch's lair. Woodcutter Kayne's skycraft, which had been hovering above the lair moments before, kicked into high gear and made a hasty U-turn. Throttles at full blast, it darted through the air, nozzle angled high. The Wicked Witch's black cloud followed. The plan was working.

Amber straightened up from her hiding position, crouched in ash-dirt behind a granite boulder outside the Wicked Witch's lair. Wolf was close beside her. They were the first wave of the attack, so to speak. She flexed her fingers before hitting the blue crystals on each of her gloves. The network's forcefield sprang up around her, forming a cocoon. The electromagnetic energy in the cocoon pulsated like a distinctly malevolent entity. It was dark, very dark. Sweat started to prickle along Amber's spine and her fingers trembled inside the gloves. This time she was completely on her own. The firewall's encryption meant that any telecoms apparatus wouldn't work within its barriers.

Swiping her hands left to right then back again, she slowly moved through the multi-layered network. She'd expected to encounter the menacing firewall immediately on entry and was a little put out that that didn't happen. The painstaking scrolling through waves of data got tiresome pretty fast. Heavy on the body, it made her arm and leg muscles work overtime. But as she continued to scroll deeper into the mass of electrons, she realised her mistake. She *was* facing it – right now. All of it was, in fact, the firewall. The minute she'd stepped into the network, the spirals of electrons she'd dismissed as nothing more than meshes of data began to swarm around her. These rapidly morphed, taking form and shape. Cyber critters.

They rushed at her all at once.

'Help!' she breathed, her voice echoing in visible ripples. It was a whopper of a task. There could be no trial and error. It would have to be one shot or nothing. If she missed just once she'd be shredded!

This thought, the intensity of her situation, should have turned her into a trembling mess of nerves. Yet, oddly enough, a considerable, comforting calm settled over her.

The cyber critters ripped viciously through data

waves around her, their fearsome forms gurgling and swooshing. In her mind, Amber found herself back in Mr Maguire's Computing class. The exact moment when she'd lacked the courage to answer a simple question. Her downcast eyes, the sense of inadequacy and fear; all of it came back to her now. She couldn't let those feelings win again. She wouldn't allow herself to fail and let everyone down, as she'd let herself down countless times.

Lifting her chin, she looked straight ahead. Arms outstretched, she harnessed the currents of electrons surrounding her. The forcefield went straight through her. It formed an energetically flaming fireball. Moulding this great mass, she lifted it high, then clenched its core. Using every ounce of strength she had, she applied as much pressure as possible. Finally, with a blinding blast, the nucleus detonated. In a single explosion, it incinerated the cyber critters.

Amber crumpled to the ground, drained. The firewall that had surrounded her spurted and faded away. All that was left were wispy embers and the billowing dust of the Wizen Plains.

Randall rushed to her side.

'You did it, Amber-Ramber! You brought down the firewall.' Cradling her, he checked her vitals. 'Heart rate's coming down, nice and steady!'

'Really?' Amber gave a shaky smile. 'I feel like my heart should've properly stopped by now.' Sitting up, she asked teasingly, 'What's next?'

Hans and G were already on it, moving stealthily towards the bunker. Camouflaged head-to-toe in khaki, they blended in with the dusky sands of the dune. Spiked boots helped their ascent up the towering mound of dirt. When they reached the top, as expected, the titanium hatch gleamed up at them, shiny beneath the layers of dust. It was just like the projection image back at the workshop; just like it had been all those years ago when they lost their way.

'You have the unlocking trijector?' Hans asked.

'Of course.' G dug into the pockets of her hoodie before presenting the hexagonal metal tool.

'Right. Let's do this then.'

Hans watched as his sister carefully set the device down, dead in the centre of the hatch. Then they waited. And waited …

'Is it working?' G whispered furiously.

Hans shrugged. 'I didn't hear anything. Maybe if we …' The device let out an almighty creak. In the next instant, bolts sprung loose. *Eureka!* Both children grinned. With raised hands, they signalled for the others.

Wolf came up first, with Amber and Randall right behind him.

'Do your work, my friend,' Randall said.

Wolf nodded. He leaned over the hatch, grabbing its front end. The muscles in his thick arms bulged visibly as he heaved, trying to open it. He soon broke into a sweat, teeth bared, putting all of his might into it. For a moment, Amber thought he would collapse – he looked as though he was about to burst. Then the massive cover began to lift, painfully slowly. Finally, it swung fully open.

'Excellent!' Randall grabbed Wolf by the shoulders. 'Excellent work!' He led the way down the hatch and inside.

The group found themselves at the top of a stone staircase, and they gingerly continued further down in single file. Reaching the bottom, they scanned the dank cavern. It came as a shock to everyone to find the place utterly deserted. No Wicked Witch. No Red. Just an empty cage standing wide open in the middle of the room.

But there was hardly any time to worry about such a major setback, a millisecond later, the walls began to move. Without shaking or shifting position, the bedrock slowly began to balloon and bubble.

'Er, what's happening?' G lifted her balaclava from her face.

Wolf braced himself. 'This can't be good.'

'It isn't,' Randall said.

Chapter Seventeen

A CLASSIC DUPING

One by one, huge creatures emerged from the limestone walls, crackling with static electricity.

'No way!' Amber couldn't believe it. Her mind was racing almost as fast as her heart rate. *It couldn't be!* She'd defeated them – outside, after accessing the Wicked Witch's network. She'd blown every last one of them to bits.

'Critters!' Randall yelled. 'They're critters! It's a failsafe in the firewall. It's–'

A volley of electric fire shot out from one of the beasts, cutting off his words. A barrage from all directions followed. Randall ducked. The tight formation the group had formed broke as they tried to take cover from the furious fire. Still more critters came out of the walls. A whole army.

'What do we do?' Hans cried, diving behind a chair, another attack splintered it, and he rolled across the floor to an alcove.

'Grab what you can!' Randall shouted. 'Hit at them! Aim for the centre. That's the heart of the mainframe.'

Each of them grabbed the nearest item to hand.

'Oh yeah!' Wolf shouted. 'Game time!' Whipping out his knife-like claws, and with an inborn ferocity, he barrelled at each critter that came his way. They may have been cyber critters, but he was an *actual* beast.

The twins tag teamed. Leaping from wall to wall, they were light-footed assassins, not hesitating to strike at the heart of the critters using any bits of the cluttered debris they could find. Handy really that they were in a witch's lair – there were plenty of potential weapons to choose from. Clearly ol' Witchy hadn't thought that one through!

For her part, Amber scrambled. Fighting these live critters as Randall had suggested seemed to be having little to no effect. They were ten times more aggressive than the cyber critters she'd fought earlier. Uniform in shape and size, they were great blobs of electric impulses: fiery orange, with arms and legs like mega sledgehammers. They blasted currents of sizzling electricity from their bloated bellies – their core, or the heart of them, as her uncle had said.

Can they even be held back, let alone defeated? Amber thought, as she threw yet another baking tray at one of the hearts. Whatever the answer, one thing was certain: the team needed a new strategy.

Randall seemed to read her mind, because he

149

called to her, 'Your gloves! Toss one over to me.'

Moments before getting zapped, Amber sidestepped. A close call. Too close. Pulling off her left glove, she threw it in her uncle's direction. For a heart-stopping moment, she thought the glove was going to miss the mark ... but it landed right in Randall's palm. He clutched it, giving her a small wink. Amber smiled with relief.

As Randall slipped on the glove, she caught on to what he planned to do and nodded her understanding. As one, they pressed the crystal activators.

A forcefield opened up in the middle of the room. It was identical to the one she'd used outside when first infiltrating the Wicked Witch's firewall.

'Now spin!' Randall directed. 'Circular motions – we're going to create a cyber vortex to swallow up these suckers!'

Frantically, imitating his movements, Amber started to spin. The pair made whisking motions with open palms. Faster and faster until a whirlpool started to form between them. Ear-splitting screeching ripped the air and sparks flew as the creatures furiously tried to resist being pulled towards it. Not daring to look up, Amber held on, whisking harder to counter the resistance. Just when Amber thought her hand would give way, the critters' volleys of fire shifted inwards and were redirected at themselves. Spurting, they sizzled before fully erupting into flames. The wild blaze surged upwards. Higher and higher, yet still, Amber didn't stop. Neither did Randall. Together, they whisked even more forcefully. Harder and faster until the fires were slowly sucked into the vortex.

When the last of the flames passed through the swirling eddy, Randall yelled, 'Shut it down!'

Amber didn't need to be told twice. She clenched her hand into a fist, disconnecting the forcefield instantly.

'Argh!' she cried, trying to catch her breath. A mixture of exhaustion and relief surged through her. As the vortex closed, sealing in the flaming critters, she staggered towards her uncle. 'We did it! We really did it!'

But Randall, equally depleted, equally breathless, was staring in horror at something just behind her. A shadow expanded from one corner. A billow of smoke had escaped through the closing gap. Amber was right in its path.

'Amber!' Randall called. 'Look out!'

Amber's smile fell away as she saw the smoke coming at her. She knew instantly that it was going to hit her. As she braced for the blow, her uncle reacted with lightning speed. He threw himself between her and the smoke. It struck him directly in the chest.

Amber watched the blackness spread over his chest, worming its way into his entire body. As the smoke seeped into his skin, Randall fell to the stone floor in a heap.

Amber dropped to her knees beside him.

'Randall? Randall!' She held him, as the others formed a shocked semicircle around them. 'Uncle! Uncle Randall, are you okay?'

His face had turned a sickly grey colour, his body cold to the touch.

'A hex … in the smoke …' His voice shook so much that he could barely get the words out. 'I should've known … should've prepared …'

'It's alright. It's just a bad shock you've had, that's all. You're fine.'

'Sorry, dear child. N-not so. It's only a matter of time …'

'No! That's not true. We can–'

'Please, Amber, you have to … to l-listen. In your back pocket … a bracelet. There's … a spare Angelpyrite attached to it …'

Amber's vision blurred, her eyes swimming in tears. She shook her head. 'What? What are you saying?'

'Put on the bracelet, child.' Her uncle's hand felt ice cold as he clasped her arm. 'Lead. See the mission through. I … I …' But his eyelids drooped shut before he could finish the sentence. His body spasmed, then went totally stiff.

Amber sobbed. A deathly quiet hung in the air. The tumultuous commotion that had shook the cavern only moments before had now ended and everything was perfectly still. Nothing and no one stirred. Only the choked sounds from Amber's throat gave any sign of life.

As the pause stretched, Wolf placed a comforting hand on Amber's shoulder.

'What can be done?' she asked, looking up at him desperately. 'How can we get him back?'

'He's in a severe state of petrification, pretty much turned to stone,' Wolf replied. 'I canny say ...'

'Surely there must be something!'

Silence.

Hans cleared his throat. 'There might be.'

All eyes turned to him.

'Think about it. All curses and spells follow the same pattern. I mean, there are common threads, right? Isn't there a way to mess with this pattern?'

'As in break the thread?' Wolf thought for a moment. 'Hmm. Chromosomes in the hex link the curse together. If we interrupt that link ...'

'We break the curse!' Amber gasped. She wiped her eyes and quickly stood. 'How do we do it?'

Wolf shifted his weight. 'A potion strong enough

could sever the link. With the emphasis on *could*.'

'And can you make such a potion?' she asked.

'Can take a crack at it! For the Prof's sake, yeah.'

Through the deep gloomy fog of grief, a ray of hope began to break through. 'Do it, Wolf,' said Amber. 'Make the potion. What do you need?'

'Not here, lass. The Wicked Witch could be back at any second. And there's still no word from the sheriff.'

'He's right.' G stood at the counter in the kitchen area, examining its contents. 'These cupcakes are freshly baked. She'll be back for them.'

'Lemme take the Prof to Evadne. We'll need to be quick, though. If the potion is not administered in the next hour, his state could be permanent, I'm afraid.' Wolf was already reaching over to pick Randall up. 'The workshop should have all that's needed to make an antidote. I'm sure you can handle things here, Amber.'

A wave of panic rushed over Amber.

'It's what the Prof would want,' Wolf said. 'He believes in you, wee one. We all do.'

Hans and G gave firm nods of agreement.

'Let's get Red back and put an end to this nightmare,' Wolf said.

Easily, as if lifting a weightless barrel, he picked Randall up and carefully slung him over one shoulder. 'Do what your uncle said. Use the bracelet. You've got this,' he said, saluting her before striding away.

Trembling, Amber reached into her back pocket. Just as Randall had said, she found a bracelet with an Angelpyrite gemstone attached. Snapping it onto her wrist felt like bonding with destiny. It gave her the courage she needed.

She had to made sure Red was rescued. Amber was the only member of Presto! left who could do it. She might be new to this world, but she had trained with Randall and had even come to know some of the secrets that were contained in the Hidden Realms. She was more than equipped and capable of seeing this mission through – right to the winning end.

She turned to face Hans and G with determination. 'Like Wolf said, let's end this nightmare.' Hands placed on her hips, she stood firm, ready for anything. 'Right. We start with a search here. Look for clues that might tell us where the Wicked Witch has taken Red.'

'I've been having a quick nose around,' Hans said. 'Not a shred of anything yet.'

'There has to be something,' Amber said, casting her eyes around the lair. Time was ticking. They couldn't risk being caught here by the Wicked Witch. But they couldn't waste this opportunity.

'What's this?' G asked. She had moved to the cluttered table where something gleamed. Reaching over, she pulled it out. 'This looks exactly like the ring Father gave to Rosina.' The gold wedding band with a heart-shaped sapphire stone glimmered brighter still as she held it up to the light.

'And these cupcakes …' Hans frowned, glancing over the kitchen countertop. 'They're just like the ones Rosina loves to make.'

A further look revealed something even more startling. Behind a fabric partitioning next to the table was an entire closet space. In it were more of Rosina's belongings: nearly half of the dresses, shoes, brushes and other items were hers, all bunched together with the Wicked Witch's things. As if Rosina and the Wicked Witch were one and the same person!

All three children's eyes widened.

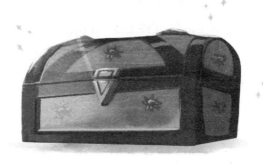

Chapter Eighteen

RED RAID

Red and the Wicked Witch were on the move. In the centre of a whirl of transparent smoke, they were cloaked in magic invisibility. As soon as she'd heard sounds of an engine above her bunker, the Wicked Witch hadn't wasted a second in deploying one of her most trusted critters.

'Buttress will deal with it,' she'd said confidently.

'I don't have time for nonsense.'

The mishapen critter, hidden in a storm cloud, had emerged from the walls, rising straight through the ceiling while Red remained caged and bound.

The Wicked Witch didn't try to enter his cage again. Instead, she held a cupcake out in front of him. 'Try one of my delicious cupcakes,' she said.

'No, thanks,' said Red. 'Funnily enough, I'm not feeling hungry right now. What with being stuck in a cage and all.'

'It wasn't a request,' said the Wicked Witch. A cruel smile played on her lips.

She waved her hand and Red felt his mouth open all by itself. He watched in horror as the cake floated into the air, glided straight through the bars of the cage and sailed into his mouth – whole. There was nothing he could do. His eyes watered as the soft, sugary taste filled his mouth. He gasped for air as it continued to slide all the way down his throat. The moment the cupcake found its way into his stomach, wooziness hit him.

'That's it, Little Red,' the Wicked Witch cackled

delightedly. 'Let the potion take over. This is my most potent one yet! Mind-controlled children are just so much easier to put up with, wouldn't you agree?'

Red tried his hardest to resist. He blinked rapidly and shook his head vigorously to try and get rid of the dense fog that was filling his head. It was no use. He was trapped in a cloudy haze that clogged up his mind and seemed to be growing thicker by the second. The fog slithered further and further into Red's mind, pulling him under until he was completely submerged. He shut his eyes and let the fog take over.

'How do you feel?'

Red opened his eyes to see the Wicked Witch bending over him. He sat up, and as he did he felt an electrified power surge through him. It was unlike anything he'd ever felt before.

'I feel strong,' he said. 'Ready for anything.'

'That's my good boy,' the Wicked Witch cooed. 'Now, are you going to do my bidding?'

In his mind's eye, Red saw the Wicked Witch's

vision for the future. The two of them stood side-by-side, ruling over the dimensions. It was incredible. He understood it now, and he knew without a doubt that he would do anything to make it happen.

'Your will is my will, Mighty Leader,' he said with a bow.

The Wicked Witch grinned. 'Then let's make it happen.'

Woodcutter Kayne darted through the clouds in his skycraft, away from the bunker. He glanced at his HUD. The black smoke that had masked his pursuer suddenly vanished to reveal something. Not the Witch, as he'd expected, but instead some kind of electro-zapping creature.

It was a decoy.

He thought of his beloved Hans and G. They were about to walk into the Wicked Witch's trap for the second time in their lives. Letting out a frustrated mutter, he grabbed the tele-communicator to warn them – a zap from the critter shook his skycraft like the worst kind of turbulence, and Woodcutter Kayne had to drop it and grab the controls to steady his course. The tele-communicator clattered to the floor and out of reach.

Shooting another glance at the HUD, he muttered to himself again. The critter was on his tail. The only option left would be to initiate grid pilot. If that couldn't free him from it, nothing would. He wished Rosina was there to whisper calming words in his ear. But right now, he was on his own, and he had to get to his children …

'Okay,' he breathed. 'And here we go.' He pushed forwards on the controls. The entire skycraft began to vibrate. The throttle blasters blazed, and it spiralled into a sudden dive, sharp and fast. Then, just as fast, the skycraft changed direction and did a complete one-eighty, soaring high up towards the sky.

The critter following behind was caught so off guard that by the time it tried to lunge back up again, its signals were scrambled, and it malfunctioned, spiralling to the ground with smoke gushing from its tail.

'Woohoo!' Woodcutter Kayne cried. He couldn't believe he'd managed to shake it off.

Now all he had to do was circle back to the lair. He just hoped he wasn't too late.

Gran Red had just ended a call with the Keepers Consortia Advisory Board. After informing them of the activity she'd seen, she was given the go-ahead to use whatever means necessary to stop the Wicked Witch. Keen not to waste another moment, she punched in the first of the codes that would open the launch pad for the cottage's cosmic blasters. Each row of letters across her virtual keyboard lit up as she tapped. A few more encryptions and the weaponry would be ready. Whatever the Wicked Witch had in store, Gran Red would be prepared as Defender of the Cosmos.

'Hi, Gran.'

Gran Red swivelled around in her chair. Red stood directly below her.

'Ah!' she cried. 'Dear boy!' Quickly releasing a lever on the side of the rocking chair, she slowly descended to the ground.

'Where have you been?' Gran Red hopped off her seat to hug her grandson. 'I was worried sick.'

'Sorry,' he said, shrugging. 'It's been mad busy at Wolf's warehouse.'

'Honestly, Wolf has a lot to answer for. That creature tests my patience to its limits.'

'What do you have going on up there?' Red moved to stare up at the monitors flashing crazily above them.

'Ah, there have been some strange things happening in the Cosmos,' Gran Red replied.

'What kind of strange things?'

'Unusual energetic shifts. I'm pretty sure the Wicked Witch is planning an attack on The Evergreen. I've inputted some codes that will release our torpedo blasters should she try anything.'

'Show me,' Red demanded.

Gran Red sat on her rocking chair once more. She pushed a button and a stand popped out from behind the bottom of the chair. Red jumped onto it and the pair rose back up towards the ceiling.

Gran Red leaned forwards, pointing at a pulsating neon trail on the system. 'That's where the activity is coming from. I just need to put in the final encryption code and we're good to go.'

'Do you still keep all the intergalactic codes sealed in that vault?' Red nodded towards a luminous safe that was fixed to the wall just below the ceiling.

His gran was too busy tapping in a code to answer.

'Gran!' Red said impatiently. 'Are the codes in the vault?'

'We don't need anything from in there just yet,' Gran Red said.

'Please let me help you, Gran,' Red coaxed. 'I can get the codes so that they're ready when you need them. You can never be too prepared.'

Gran Red looked at her grandson, her mouth hanging open in surprise. Red had never shown the least interest Keeper duties. He always made it clear that he'd rather be whizzing through the desert on his bike.

'It's my inheritance, after all,' Red said quickly, seeing the flabbergasted expression on her face. 'I want to be involved.'

Gran Red stared at him, a smile as wide as the moon on her face. 'You don't know how pleased I am to hear that,' she said. She turned and leaned towards the vault, which could only be opened by eye recognition.

As soon as the eye scan was confirmed, the vault clicked open. A blow struck Gran Red from behind, knocking her out of her chair and sending her tumbling headfirst towards the floor.

Gran Red could not believe it. He'd shoved her. Red had shoved her!

Trembling with shock, Gran Red rolled over to her side and pushed herself up into a side-sitting position. Red was stationed comfortably in her chair and was typing away furiously on her systems.

What in the Cosmos?

Then, as Gran Red crawled towards the sofa to pull herself up, a cloud of smoke slinked out of the floor, spreading out horizontally. Gran Red stared in terror.

'Hello, Eireen. How have you been?'

The smoke morphed into a long white mane around a hard angular face shadowed by a dark satin hood.

'Nina!' Gran Red gasped. 'Is that you?'

Over fifty years had passed since she'd last seen her former best friend. The woman in front of her now had not aged at all. There wasn't a wrinkle on her beautiful stony face. Gran Red did not want to imagine the dark rituals that had been used to maintain such youth.

Nina gave her a small wink. 'Hi there, traitor. It's been too long, old friend.'

Chapter Nineteen

YEARS GONE BY

Fifty years earlier

It was the year of their sixteenth birthdays.
Graduation from Keeper Academy was only a week
away and everybody was busy finalising plans. With
gown designs, guest lists and after-party particulars
to be planned, excitement echoed through the

Common Room and the surrounding corridors.

Nina and Eireen lounged on a sofa, their legs intertwined, Nina's posse of followers lying on the floor around them.

'Just wait until you see some of the things Mother has come up with for the after ceremony,' one of the girls was saying. 'It's almost *too* much!' She laughed, and the others joined in.

'Tell me about it,' giggled another. 'My father is planning on turning our whole house into a shrine, judging by the number of picture frames he's got for the graduation photos.'

Cue more laughter.

Irritation had been bubbling up in Nina all day. Now it sparked into hot anger. 'Just shut up about it already!' she shouted.

The entire room fell quiet.

'You all make me sick!' Nina stood and stomped towards the veranda with an unquenchable fury burning inside her. Yanking open the double doors, she let the crisp night air cool her face. She leaned over the railings and looked up at the sky. A lovely starry evening. Just like the night her mother had abandoned her, dropping her at the gates of Keeper Academy as a six-year-old before leaving forever.

'Are you okay?' Eireen asked, coming up behind her. Nina smiled, blinking back tears. Unlike the fake hangers-on that swarmed around Nina, Eireen remained true; ever pure … good.

Now, there was a word. *Good*. She longed for Eireen's kindness and graciousness. Yet she just didn't have it in her. However much she tried, it seemed the opposite of good ran through her veins.

'I'm fine,' she said to Eireen, and took a deep breath. 'Sorry, I shouldn't have reacted like that. But all that talk about parents and families … it got to me.'

'I understand.' Eireen placed a comforting hand on her arm.

Nina sighed. 'You know my mother left me on a night just like this one?' she said. 'She told me she would be right back.'

Eireen moved to stand beside her, and Nina rested her head on her shoulder.

'She couldn't cope,' Nina went on. 'She'd run away from my father, but I was a constant reminder of him. They say he was the son of a powerful dark lord. When Mama realised who she'd gotten involved with, she didn't want any part of it. Not even me.' As she spoke, a scorching pain spiked inside Nina.

It was too hot to put out.

By the time Graduation Day arrived, Nina's rage was a flaming furnace she could barely control.

As she watched the happy families gathering all around her, something snapped. She crept into the headteacher's quarters and stole the key to the Keeper Academy's basement. Down and down and down the winding steps she went, until she reached the locked door to the basement. Ignoring the *OUT OF BOUNDS* sign, she slipped the key into the lock and pushed open the door.

As the prime centre of learning in the Cosmos, the Keeper Academy trained its students to defeat the dangerous forces that they would face once they became Keepers. For the rest of the time, these forces were safely locked away in the basement.

Nina stepped inside the dark room, and the twisting rage inside her found a focus. She would release the imprisoned lethal forces, guaranteeing a night of mayhem no one would ever forget. The aching hurt in her chest would finally have an outlet at last.

She approached the glass panels that held the dark matter. One flick of a switch was all it would take.

'Nina?'

Eireen hurried into the room. Her voice trailed off as she saw Nina's hand poised near the enclosure switch. 'What are you doing?'

'Perfect timing!' Nina was genuinely pleased to see her friend. They could share in the moment together. After all, Eireen was the only person who truly got her. 'Can you imagine everyone's faces if we released these?'

But Eireen's expression was not what she'd expected. Her friend was horrified.

'You can't be serious. It could destroy the whole school!'

'And?' Nina laughed. 'This place is a dump anyway. I hated it the moment I was left here, and I still hate it now.'

'Nina ...' Eireen took a small step forward. 'I can only imagine what it's been like for you. But doing this won't help.' She slowly moved closer.

Nina swallowed. Tears welled in her eyes, and she furiously rubbed them. 'Well, I think it will.'

'Please!'

Nina shook her head.

'No!' Eireen pleaded. 'This is not the person you want to be.'

'Maybe it's who I already am.'

As Nina reached for the switch, Eireen leaped and pushed her friend to the ground. Pinning her down, she hit an alarm bell that was next to the glass panels. The deafening ringing pierced the air as red lights flashed. It almost drowned out the click of additional security engaging around the enclosure – there would be no opening it now. Nina furiously tried to shove Eireen away. They struggled, rolling across the floor.

'It's over,' Eireen breathed. 'There's nothing you can do!'

With a cry of rage, Nina broke free. 'You traitor!' she spat. 'You'd better pray that our paths never cross again.'

As Nina ran for the door, her heart broke. She had no interest in putting the pieces back together again. Who needed a heart when even your best friend didn't understand you. Feelings just let you down. The time had come for her to embrace her father's heritage. She would make her way to the dark dimensions and learn the ways of the dark arts. Let the blackness fill her instead of goodness. She would become more powerful than anyone could ever imagine and inflict the hurt and pain she felt right now on the rest of the world. No one, not even Eireen, would be spared.

Chapter Twenty

CLUES AND CONCLUSIONS

Bobby looked around to make sure that no one was watching him. He didn't want to get caught breaking into the professor's flat. He had discovered the balcony doors weren't locked, so he wasn't even sure that it counted as breaking and entering. Surely everyone would understand his wanting to get to the bottom of the sinister goings on in the flat. What could that sham professor be up to? And just how did he and that niece of his seemingly vanish into thin air?

Taking a deep breath, Bobby stepped into the living room. Like a detective at a crime scene, he looked around intently, examining anything and everything. On the TV screen – that had so carelessly been left on – was a moving, pixelating soft orange glow. Had these people not heard of reducing carbon dioxide emissions? Honestly! How big was their carbon footprint? It was just as well he was here. He would do his bit to save the planet, even if that ridiculous professor thought he was above it all.

His gaze fell onto the remote control lying on the far side of the coffee table. The thing was so ginormous that it must consume a factory's worth of energy. He snatched it up and pointed it at the screen. But when he pushed what he assumed was the power button, rather than turning off, the screen seemed to grow brighter. Light flooded around him.

Bobby let out a cry and dropped the remote. As it hit the carpeted floor, he took a step towards the screen. The growing light intensified into dazzling rays. He stumbled forwards, unable to see; everything became a blinding brilliance. And a split second later, he let out an undignified screech as he found himself being sucked directly into the screen.

For the briefest moment he felt a warm and tingling sensation, then nothing.

Bobby waited, breath held and body tensed for a blow, a crash – something. He didn't dare open his eyes. But when nothing came and the seconds ticked away, he slowly peeled apart his eyelids – and almost wished he hadn't. Wherever he'd ended up, it was a far cry from Professor Abeiro's living room. A banner above an entranceway read: *PRESTO! MAGICAL RECOVERY CO.* What on earth was that when it was at home?

'Who are you?'

Nearly jumping out of his skin at the voice, Bobby snapped round sharply. He came face to face with what could only be described as the strangest monstrosity he'd ever seen. An enormous wolf-like creature stood in front of him, decked out in a full tartan kilt!

'Oh, geez!' Bobby cried. 'Geez it!' He tried to back away into the screen. Unfortunately for him, it had become nothing more than a reflective slate. No flashing lights, no TV, just an inanimate mirrored surface.

A thousand percent panicked, Bobby anxiously shuffled from side to side.

'Oh, nervous, are we? Big Bad Wolf scaring you? Should we fix that?' Bobby watched in horror as the creature flexed its huge muscles before shapeshifting into a human. 'This better?' it asked. 'Or this …?' Another rapid shapeshift into a lamb, then a kitten, then back to his original bulky self. 'Nah, will keep as is.'

Eyes bulging at this point, Bobby cried out. 'Whoa! Whoa! Stay back,' he commanded, holding his hands up in front of him. 'Far back, demon!'

Totally unfazed, the creature only looked at him. 'I've had my fill of hysterical children, thank you very much,' it scoffed. 'No mucking about with jitters anymore. Care to tell me who you are, lad, and what your business here is?'

'I – the pr-professor,' Bobby stammered. 'I'm his neighbour, Bobby.'

'Ah! The soppy snoop from earlier. Thought we'd got rid of you, but turns out you're right resourceful, aren't you? Needed that wee curiosity fix, eh? Well, "Bobby the neighbour", you have great timing. We're gonna put you to good use!'

'I-I just really need to be getting on home ...' Bobby stuttered.

He might as well have saved his breath for the amount of notice the creature took. Wolf moved over to a countertop and started to tip and mix test tubes over a burner. Bobby was about to protest further when he noticed a familiar figure not too far from where the creature stood concocting its potions.

Professor Abeiro!

Laid out across a settee, completely motionless, was his landlord and neighbour. Bobby's heart thumped. 'That's the professor! What have you done to him?' he cried. *Oh, geez. Geez, geez, geez!* What exactly had he got himself mixed up in here? Bobby had long suspected his landlord to be a criminal weirdo, but this … It was too much.

'*I* didn't do anything,' Wolf said. 'He's been cursed – a petrification spell. There isn't time to explain. You're a heaven-send, Bobby. I'm going to need you to find an important ingredient for the antidote for me.'

Bobby didn't know whether to laugh or cry. *As if!* He most certainly would not be getting anything for anyone. Right now, getting home was the only thing he was interested in.

'No. Sorry, I can't. I won't be involved in this.'

'You already are, laddie. Grab these.'

Without thinking, Bobby caught the set of keys tossed at him.

'We have one shot at saving the Prof's life,' the beast went on. 'We *must* have the final ingredient. My workers are on their way from our warehouse. They'll drive you. I'll give you a map showing the exact location of the root plant we need. Speed is key.' Wolf grinned at him, revealing a ferocious set of teeth. 'You onboard, Bobby Boy? Saving a man's life is the neighbourly thing to do, after all.'

Bobby rolled his eyes. It didn't look as if he had much choice.

'How could we have missed this?' G cried, putting a palm to her forehead.

Hans shook his head in bewilderment. 'How did she fool us?'

'To be fair,' Amber said, 'she probably used magic to keep you guys from realising exactly who she is.'

'But how?' asked Hans. 'We'd have noticed if she was muttering spells around us.'

Both of the twins' gazes fell on the cakes again. 'The cupcakes,' they said as one.

'I bet they're enchanted,' said G.

'No wonder she did so much baking,' added Hans. 'She had to keep us all dosed up, so we wouldn't see the real her.'

Deflated, G leaned back against a wall. She jumped away when it shifted beneath her weight. 'What in the world?'

Part of the limestone creased into a faint outline, forming a rectangular shape.

'It looks like a doorway!' Hans gasped.

If it looks like a duck, walks like a duck and quacks like a duck … Amber thought. She pushed against the outline with both hands. Hans and G joined in, and a few heaves later, the three of them managed to move the stone. It gave way, opening up to what was clearly a hidden chamber.

The three children piled into the space.

'Wow,' Amber breathed.

A ceiling-to-floor mural hung heavy and wide. It was a massive diagram showing the whole of Evadne in vividly coloured pictures. Arrow markings plotted a direct pathway through the different regions of the land.

Amber moved closer. 'See this pathway here? It starts right there, in the Plains.' She traced her finger along the varnished surface of the drawing.

'And moves along through The Evergreen.'

'There's a circle around that part there.' G pointed to the area.

'That's the Glass Cottage,' Hans said. 'Gran Red's place.'

'Of course!' Amber nodded, everything clicking into place in her mind. 'That's why Rosina kidnapped Red. She needs him to access the cottage!'

'And that's why she baked more cupcakes,' G said. 'I've read about this type of thing before, in one of Father's Forestry Department books. It's a type of spell. She's obviously using mind control to get him to do it.'

'The Glass Cottage has some of the most powerful codes in the Cosmos!' Hans exclaimed. 'Can you imagine what someone like Rosina could do with them?'

Amber shuddered. 'We have to get to Gran Red. I could use the Teleportation Element to get us there from the lake near your house.'

G frowned. 'But if Red's already there with the Wicked Witch and under her spell, aren't we too late?'

'Maybe,' Amber replied. 'But didn't you say Rosina needed to be constantly dishing up her pastries to keep your family under her control? I'm sure at some point her charms on Red are going to start wearing off. If we can get to him by then, we might just have a chance of rescuing him.'

'Wait!' G raised a hand. 'Do you hear something?'

Amber did. The noise was coming from above and grew gradually louder. It was the whirring of a skycraft.

Chapter Twenty-One

LOOPY LOOTINGS

As arranged in planning, Woodcutter Kayne skilfully brought the skycraft down a few metres away from the bunker, having effectively carried out the decoy mission. Turning off the engine, he stepped out of the craft. He was met by the three children who'd heard the distinctive whir of the engine from inside the bunker. Relieved to see them safe, he scooped up the twins into a huge bear hug.

'Am I glad to see you!' he cried. 'Are you alright?'

He glanced towards Amber, who was thoughtfully tapping at the bracelet Randall had given her.

'We're fine, Papa.' G held on to him tightly. 'So glad to see you too.' Hans puffed out a breath as they broke the embrace. 'We've had a bit of a time of it!'

'So have I,' the Woodcutter said. 'Didn't think I'd ever shake that beastly thing. And it wasn't her by the way, the Wicked Witch. Just a decoy she set off to divert me.'

'We know,' Hans said. 'She tricked us all.'

'And that's not the half of it,' G added. 'There's something you should see.'

Woodcutter Kayne gave his daughter a quizzical look as she reached into a pocket and brought out a ring. He recognised it straight away.

'What are you doing with Rosina's ring?'

'She lives here, Papa,' G said, handing over the wedding band.

'Nonsense! How can she live here? There's

nothing around here, except dusty dunes.' He looked to the bunker behind them. 'Also, Rosina's been part of our home since you were little. What do you mean she lives here?' He looked at his children, puzzled.

'Rosina isn't who she made herself out to be,' Hans said gently. 'She's the Wicked Witch.'

The Woodcutter couldn't believe it – *wouldn't* believe it. 'No ...' His voice was low, just that single word, with so much contained in it. His mind was racing.

'It's true, Papa!' G cried. 'She's been in disguise since we met her. She uses mind control potions in her cakes and pastries to keep us from fully seeing anything.'

Woodcutter Kayne was a well-built man who'd been on the frontline fighting crime for a long time, but the news almost caused his knees to give way from under him. 'Are you certain?' he asked, sounding strained.

Amber gave a sympathetic nod. 'And I'm afraid it gets worse.'

'You mean there's something worse than finding out my entire life is a lie? Go on. How much worse?'

Bobby could have done without these ridiculous cubs who called themselves the 'Loopy Looters'. It was proving to be a non-stop chore trying to keep them in line. Since that wolf-person-thingy had sent them all off on this horrid errand, the cubs had pretty much run riot. The professor would owe him *big* after this one!

Just the thought of the contraption he was currently on made Bobby's stomach turn. Scrappy, metallic thing, it looked as if it would come apart at the least bump in the road. But Bobby had had little choice other than to climb onto the back of it and cling on for dear life to his Loopy Looters driver.

Rocketing out of the workshop's parking area, they careened onto the glistening streets of the city. Cracking his eyelids open a fraction, even Bobby had to admit that this Evadne place *was* magical.

He wished he'd had his mobile on him when he'd snuck into Apartment 1A. Photographic evidence was needed. No one back home would believe him if he told them!

Soon, Bobby and his entourage of looters left the spectacular city behind, heading at speed through the outskirts. Wolf had said a simple root was the essential ingredient to Randall Abeiro's *un*-petrifying potion. Allegedly, it grew in the thickets of a forest called The Evergreen, and it held special properties that would be key to breaking the spell.

Bobby had the map of the area memorised. And, judging from where they were currently, provided he remembered the map details correctly, they were halfway there.

His impatience increased. The sooner they got that root back to Wolf, the sooner he could return home and put this whole horrid mess behind him. Gulping in breaths of air, he had just about steadied his nerves when a sudden shift unravelled the whole process. Out of the blue, a very large, very solid obstruction positioned itself directly in their path

… and his cub driver crashed right into it!

Woodcutter Kayne had just landed in The Evergreen when a forceful thud suddenly jarred the skycraft.

'Something's hit us from behind!' he shouted.

Amber was already clambering out of the aircraft, with Hans and G fast behind her. Woodcutter Kayne was right. The mangled scene in front of them indicated a crash. A gang of cubs were pulling someone out of the wreckage, before reaching for someone else. Amber gaped as a slight boy with a short Afro was hauled from beneath the debris. Luckily, there didn't seem to be a scratch on him.

'Bobby!' she cried, recognising him immediately. Who could forget someone that irritating? 'What are you doing here?'

'Oh, the delightful niece,' he said, grimacing. 'No suitcases this time?'

Amber decided to ignore his sarcasm. 'Again, what are you doing here?'

'Are you okay?' Woodcutter Kayne stepped between them.

'Ah, finally, someone seems to actually care.' Bobby threw his hands in the air dramatically. 'Thank you, kind sir. I seem to be in one piece!'

'You know, you really shouldn't be here,' Amber said.

'I'll just leave your uncle to his demise, shall I then?'

'How do you have anything to do with my uncle?' Her voice was high-pitched with agitation.

'I happen to be the only one standing between him and eternal petrification.'

'So, you've been to the workshop?' Amber struggled to follow. 'You've spoken to Wolf?'

'He says there's a final ingredient needed for the antidote and he couldn't get it himself. Just call me your hero!'

Amber rolled her eyes, unable to imagine anyone *less* like a hero.

'Amber,' G said. 'If he's okay, we should leave him to it, and get moving. We're wasting time here.'

G was right. If Bobby had to be the person to get the final ingredient that Wolf needed to complete the antidote, then they had no choice but to trust him.

'Fine,' Amber said. 'Let's get you set up on another scooter, Bobby. There isn't a moment to lose.'

Chapter Twenty-Two

COLLISION

Amber hoped they weren't too late. She, Hans, G and Woodcutter Kayne watched as beams of energy surged upwards from Gran Red's roof.

Something was definitely amiss.

'I'll take care of Rosina,' Woodcutter Kayne said. 'The rest of you should get Red and his gran out of there.'

It didn't seem like much of a plan, but what else could they do?

They had to do something – and fast, Amber thought.

Whatever chaos the Wicked Witch had unleashed, it would likely be in the main living space. This was where the twins had said Gran Red usually ran her operations for the Consortia of Keepers.

Moving swiftly, silently, they advanced on the building. At the back entrance a locked gate with a flashing dial pad barred their way.

'We need a code to get in,' Hans said.

Amber's heart sank. 'But we can't give up now!' she said. 'We've got this far.'

'Well, lucky for us, we have this,' Hans said with a wink, producing the unlocking trijector they'd used to get into the Wicked Witch's bunker.

Moments later, the gate buzzed open. The noise and blasts of energy beams intensified. Slowly, they crept in through the back door of the cottage. Voices could be heard coming from the living room.

'If you look at it from a technical point of view,'

someone was saying, 'I didn't lie at all. Rosina *is* my full name. My mama shortened it to Nina.'

Woodcutter Kayne walked up behind his wife. 'So, it really is you, Rosina,' he said, shaking his head. 'How could you?'

Rosina whirled round. 'I was doing it for us,' she said. 'Please don't hate me. I couldn't bear it if I lost you too. With the Keeper codes in my possession, I'll be completely in charge. Just think, we can–'

Amber nudged Hans and G, who were transfixed by the scene playing out between their father and stepmother. 'We need to find Red,' she hissed. Hans nodded, and with a last look over their shoulders, the twins followed Amber further into the cottage. She had never seen anything like it. Various types of flowers and plants were arranged across every surface, but most astonishing and remarkable of all was the ceiling. It was like some huge display screen, from end-to-end twinkling starlit skies shimmered, burning with a distant brilliance. It took her breath away.

Just below the star ceiling, there was a young

boy perched on a high-tech rocking chair, straight-backed and furiously typing. With each stroke of the keyboard, a portal above him opened up ever wider. Judging from the filthy red hoodie he was wearing; it could only be Red Riding Hood.

'Hey!' Amber hissed, trying to get the boy's attention. He didn't so much as blink; he just continued with his frenzied typing.

'Red!' she tried again. Still no reaction.

'It's no use,' G whispered. 'He's obviously under an enchantment.'

'We can thank our lovely stepmother for that,' Hans added, looking over to where Rosina was still arguing with the twins' father.

Amber stared frantically around the room, looking for something – anything – that would help them. Suddenly, her attention was caught by an older woman with curly grey hair, clutching her side, in obvious pain. She was waving desperately, and pointing at something just behind Amber, yet making sure Rosina didn't spot her movements. From what Amber could tell, this had to be Gran

Red. Amber turned to see what she was pointing at; it was a large ornate chest set against the wall. Glancing back at the woman she was now sure was Red's grandmother, Amber raised her eyebrows.

'This?' she mouthed, pointing at the chest.

Gran Red nodded back and made an opening motion with her hands.

Careful not to draw attention to herself, Amber crept over to the chest and knelt beside it.

Please, please, please don't creak! she thought, as she grasped the lid with both hands. Luck was on her side, and the chest opened without a sound. Amber peered inside. Inside lay a bright red cape. Amber grabbed it. She had no idea what a mere cape could do, but at this point she was ready to try anything. Slowly, hardly daring to breathe, Amber took step after careful step towards Gran Red. It was like that game she used to play at school, where everyone had to sneak up behind the person playing 'grandmother' without getting caught. Only this time the stakes were much, much higher. Amber dreaded to think what Rosina might do if she spotted her. Turn her into a frog? Lock her away in a tower? Her mind was awash with thoughts of all the terrible things witches had done in the fairy tales she had read as a small child; it made her legs shake and wobble beneath her. Finally, she was within touching distance of Gran Red. Exhaling softly, she held out the cape.

In one swift movement, Gran Red snatched the cape from Amber and flung it at Rosina. Before the witch could react, the folds of the material wrapped themselves tightly around her.

'What have you done?' Rosina shrieked and struggled, but the cape remained firmly in place. She couldn't move at all.

'That, my *dear* friend, is a clamping cloak.' Gran Red grinned. 'Try casting spells in that!'

Ignoring Rosina's squawks and squeals, Gran Red turned to the others. 'We have to stop Red!' She pointed to a cupboard in the corner. 'There's a stepladder in there,' she said.

Amber dashed to grab it. The ladder seemed far too small to ever reach Red. But, as she quickly put it against the wall, it stretched out and kept on going – right up into the twinkling star ceiling.

A magic elongating ladder! As she stared up it, Amber wondered again if this world would ever stop surprising her. She definitely didn't think so. The Woodcutter kept a firm hold on the now bound Rosina, as Gran Red steadied herself on an armchair. The twins held the ladder for Amber.

Amber clambered up the rungs without hesitation. Once she was close enough to Red, she knocked the keyboard away from his clutches. But another instantly appeared in its place, and Red simply carried on his frenzied inputting of code.

'Pesky magic,' Amber muttered. Moving position, she managed to clamp her arms around the boy and tried to pull him away from the keyboard. He wouldn't budge. Bewitched people seemed to have the strength of ten dozen wrestlers!

Holding firmly onto his hood, Amber tugged as hard as she could. Which was maybe a little too hard, as moments later the two of them were tumbling towards the ground. Together, they hit the floor with a thud. Amber had never hurt so much in her life. She had just about struggled into a sitting position when, to add insult to injury, Red threw up all over her.

'Ew!' she moaned, as the twins helped her up. 'I smell like mouldy cupcakes.'

Red, meanwhile, was looking around in confusion. 'What's going on? Where am I?'

'You're safe, dear boy,' Gran Red said, as she folded her arms around him. 'You're finally safe.'

'And that?' Woodcutter Kayne had eyes on the vortex still swirling chaotically above them. 'How do we undo that?'

'It's too late,' Rosina cackled. 'The portal's already been opened. Dimensions are intersecting and colliding as we speak.'

Amber stared at her in horror. It couldn't be too late. It just couldn't. Had they done all this for nothing?

202

One of Wolf's cubs dropped Bobby off outside Presto! Magical Recovery Co., and he ran into the lift, Bobby clung tightly to the pouch containing the fabled root in his hand. It had been no easy task, but after scouring the hills of The Evergreen, he'd finally found it.

'What's happening?' he asked Wolf, gesturing at the windows where the sky and city below faded in and out, as though they were disappearing. It was like a glitch in a video game.

'There's no time to explain, we need to act fast.' Wolf held out a hand. 'The root?'

Bobby sulkily handed over the pouch. 'You're welcome,' he said drily.

Wolf paid him no mind, already occupied with emptying the contents into a beaker. When the root dissolved into the concoction, Wolf hurried over to the settee where Randall lay, terrifyingly still.

'Help me sit him up,' he told Bobby.

Bobby did as he was told. After a few hefty heaves, he was able to get Professor Abeiro into a sitting position, more or less. Wolf parted Randall's lips before pouring the entire contents of the beaker down his throat.

For a beat, nothing happened. Then Randall jerked, gasping awake.

Wolf grinned. 'Welcome back, Prof!'

Randall took deep gulping breaths.

'Hiya, Professor,' Bobby added.

Randall blinked. But before he could find his voice, a flash of light in the centre of the room caught everyone's attention as Amber materialised before their eyes.

'Randall!' she cried, dashing across the workshop and wrapping her arms around him. 'You're all right!'

Randall patted her hair. 'Yes, child. I'm okay. Thanks to you all.'

The room went dark, then suddenly light again as the glitching intensified. Randall looked at Amber quizzically.

'It's the Wicked Witch,' she explained. 'She used the codes from the Glass Cottage to merge the dimensions. We couldn't stop her.'

'What about Red?' Wolf asked.

'He's safe. Gran Red managed to imprison Rosina. Woodcutter Kayne and the twins are holding her prisoner right now.'

'Hang on …' Wolf frowned. 'Why would they imprison Rosina?'

Randall jumped up, putting the pieces together. 'It's been her all along.' He breathed in, in no small amount of shock. 'Rosina is the Wicked Witch!'

Amber confirmed this with a nod.

'I'm lost.' Bobby looked confusedly from one to the other. 'Who's Rosina?"

'Never mind about that right now, dear boy,' Randall said. 'This is bad. Very bad. Whatever she's done, worlds are colliding. This could expose the Hidden Realms to Earth. And not just that: the collision could be catastrophic for both! And the Wicked Witch has missed one crucial element: misused, the codes *will* combust! Creating millions of tiny particles that will fragment the function and reality of … well, everything! The ultimate collision of the Cosmos, I'm talking a full-on merging, a jumbled mesh, fairy tale lands and Earth combined – but with everything we know, or they know turned topsy-turvy.'

Exasperated, Bobby put a palm to his forehead. 'I just want to go home!'

Amber ignored him. 'There must be something we can do?' she asked.

Randall paused, deep in thought. 'There might be. Though it would pose risks of its own.'

'Whatever it is, Prof, it better be quick,' said Wolf, eyes fixed on the darkening sky and waning city below, flickering in and out of reality.

'We need to get back to my office in Brixton. But first there's something I must tell you all. I'm so sorry, but I haven't been completely honest with you …'

Chapter Twenty-Three

DEUS MACHINA

'I think it's best I start at the beginning,' said Randall, sinking back onto the sofa and closing his eyes. 'When he was a boy, my father came across something remarkable in the jungles of Kenya. A gemstone unlike any known material on Earth. He couldn't have known it at the time, all the power harnessed within that small entity.

'He held onto it through many conflicts and hardships, and through all the political troubles that took over the country. It was his precious secret. A lucky charm. He kept it in his pocket, a source of comfort like nothing else.

'He grew old with it, still unaware of its true nature or powers. On his death bed, he left it to his three children.' Randall opened his eyes to look at Amber. 'Your father, myself and your Aunt Onya.'

Amber stared at him. She had never heard of an Aunt Onya. Her name had never been mentioned. Not by her father, not by Randall, not by anybody.

Randall nodded sadly at her. 'None of us ever talk about her. Because what happened next changed everything. Onya was undoubtedly the most brilliant of all of us. It didn't take her long to discover that the gemstone she called Angelpyrite held special properties that could be harnessed. She worked out how to use it to open a portal to other dimensions, and we all explored them with her.'

'You mean my father has been *here*?' Amber asked. She could not imagine her suited-and-booted father in this world, so far away from his natural habitat of conference rooms. The surprises just kept coming! Amber would never in a gazillion years have thought of her father as a part of anything adventurous. He'd always been such a stickler for the tangible. Things like law, books and other predictable practicalities. The most *un*-gadgety person she knew. Surely Randall was mistaken.

But Randall was adamant. 'Yup. Your father too. We started taking the odd souvenir here and there to bring back home. Rapunzel's diamond-encrusted hairbrush. A ruby necklace from Ariel's private collection. Things like that. We didn't think we were doing anything wrong. It was simply good fun. Eventually, the Consortia of Keepers got hold of us. They ordered us to return every item we'd ever taken,' Randall continued. 'When we saw how our actions had affected those we'd stolen from, it was heart-breaking. We'd divided families, caused havoc in cities, even put lives at risk.

'Onya in particular was horrified. She decided that since we'd done so much taking, we should redress the balance with some giving. It became an ongoing process of recovering stolen or missing items for anyone in the Realms who needed help. All voluntary at this stage, mind you. Eventually, there was a steady stream of work for us, and people gave us gold in return! And so, Presto! The Magical Recovery Co. was born.'

'Wow!' Amber breathed. 'But you haven't explained what happened to Onya?'

Perched on the edge of a table, Bobby shuffled. 'This is a pretty long story,' he moaned, tapping restlessly on the wooden surface.

'Hmm,' Wolf agreed, thoughtfully looking out of the glass walls at their rapidly impending doom.

'I'm getting there,' Randall assured them. 'For a while, things ran smoothly. But Onya was eager to build a bigger business. So much so that one summer she told us she wanted to stay on in the Hidden Realms full time. The world she came from just wasn't enough for her anymore.

'That was the last time we ever saw her. We don't know the details, but somehow a recovery job went wrong, and Onya was lost in one of the many Realms. We've never been able to trace her. Onya's disappearance affected your father and I in different ways. For me, it spurred me on to continue in the spirit of helping the communities of the Hidden Realms and carrying on the legacy of Presto! as Onya would have wanted. But for your father, it meant cutting ties with it all. No more inter-realm travel. No Presto!. No programming. It was easier for him, I guess, to stomp out all thought of magic from his life. We agreed to never speak of her again.'

'My father was a programmer?' Amber asked, bewildered.

'Yes, once upon a time, your father was indeed one of the finest programmers in the business,' Randall said. 'Out of us siblings, Onya was the scientist slash engineer. I was the physicist and your father was the tech whizz – programming genius some might say. I have no doubt that he still has the touch, even after all these years. And I can safely bet he's probably the only one who can get the Deus Machina working right. Him agreeing, however, is

211

a whole other matter. I'm not sure if he'd be willing to do it. As for me–'

'It's been your life's mission to bring Onya back since,' Amber finished for him, understanding now. On all the missions her uncle went on, there was always the hope that one of those trips would lead him to his sister.

Tears welled up in Amber's eyes. She felt sad for him – for her father and Onya too – but she admired his dedication and optimism.

'Onya's lucky to have you,' she said. 'You're the most brilliant person I know – if anyone can find her, you can.'

Randall's eyes shone with emotion. He gave Amber a hug.

Wolf stood up, scraping back a chair loudly, effectively cutting into the moment. 'I'm sorry for your loss there, Prof, but if we could park the tears and hugs for a bit, aye,' he said. 'The world is literally falling apart around us.' He indicated the reflective screen ready to take them back to Brixton. 'Shall we?'

With that, he stepped through the screen.

As soon as they were back in Randall's office, he hurried over to the wall.

'Amber, help me move this.' Randall stood beneath a painting. It was a depiction of an African jungle on a rainy day. Together, he and Amber unhooked the painting and set it aside, revealing a safe embedded in the wall where it had hung.

With his index finger, Randall quickly punched a number combination into the keypad beside it, cracking the safe open. He reached inside with both arms and heaved out a hefty cylindrical contraption. The softly pulsating device had all types of wires and cables attached to it, criss-crossed around it in a multicoloured mesh, like a tapestry of different materials woven together.

'Hey, aren't we missing one person?' Amber suddenly asked, remembering.

Wolf came to stand beside her. 'If you mean the

lad Bobby, last I saw he was headed out the door the moment we got to the Prof's place.'

Ha! Amber thought. *How's that? Not a word, just slinking off.* Though, to be fair to him, they had been somewhat preoccupied at the time, and he also probably didn't want to get any more involved than he already had been. He'd certainly whinged enough about going home!

'Clear the desk,' Randall directed, the weight of the contraption clearly too much of a burden for him to continue holding for long.

With Wolf's help, Amber hastily scattered everything on the desk to make enough space. Randall set down the contraption, puffing out a strained sigh.

'I've been building this machine for the last twenty years. I call it Deus Machina.'

'That means "Deity Machine" in Latin,' Wolf translated.

Randall nodded. 'I've travelled through all the fairy tale worlds of the Hidden Realms, scavenging for mythical bits and pieces to put it together.'

'It's massive!' Amber examined the intricate contraption. 'You mean to say that each part is from the Hidden Realms?'

Randall gave a nod. 'Once Presto! started getting paying customers, I wasn't always paid in good old gold. In the beginning, all manner of gifts came my way. One day, an old pedlar gave me a parchment with a blueprint as thanks. It was the blueprint to this machine right here. Built intricate piece by intricate piece.'

'No wonder it's taken you twenty years!' Wolf exclaimed.

'It's far from complete, though,' Randall said. 'But a little tweaking here and there, and it should work well enough to stop the collision of the Cosmos.'

'And what are the odds on that, Prof?' Wolf asked.

'That I don't know. It was built for a different purpose. I'm hoping if we code it in reverse, it will create electromagnetic barriers that can undo the gravitational pulls forming in the quantum landscape.'

'Once more in English?' Wolf grumbled.

'The Hidden Realms and *our* world will remain separate.'

'But what is it actually meant to do?' Amber asked.

Randall took a breath. 'To alter quantum reality.'

'Like change the present?' Wolf said.

Randall nodded. 'And the past. When it's finished.'

'You want to go back and stop Onya from disappearing,' Amber said.

'Yes.' Randall nodded. 'And this time, I would never leave her on her own.' He rubbed his eyes. 'Anyway, I'm hoping that if I also rewire it in reverse, it should act as a kind of repellent, a magic anti-seal, if you will, preventing the joining of the Cosmos.'

'Right,' said Wolf. 'Let's take this big buster back to the workshop and save our worlds!'

Chapter Twenty-Four

AN UNLIKELY HERO

Back at Presto!, the skies were angry. Lightning sparked through the clouds and the building shook with every clap of thunder as the city below faded into a barely detectable haze. The eternal sunshine of Evadne was no more. Amber was aghast at what she saw. Playing out before her eyes was the degeneration of an entire world.

'We need to act now, Professor!' Wolf yelled above the noise.

'On it!' Randall was setting up the Deus Machina as quickly as he could. 'It shouldn't take more than a moment.'

Some moments later, he sighed in frustration. 'Dithering disasters! Why won't this work?'

'Let me give it a go,' Amber said. She'd not done too badly so far, engaging with crazy new software. She might just be able to crack this too.

'No pressure,' said Wolf. 'If you can't make it work, it really is the end of the world.'

Her mouth set in a grim line, Amber got to work. The Deus Machina had an intricate mainframe that was tricksy to navigate. Tapping in symbols and keys to get data inscriptions, Amber tried to maintain a synchronised output. Once or twice, she thought she'd succeeded, only for the machine to turn up an error message.

'You may have outdone yourself here, Randall,'

she sighed. 'I'm trying, but your machine's internal drive is far too advanced.'

'You're right. Only your father can help us now, Amby. He's the only one who's more of a gadget head than either of us. But I doubt he'll be willing to do it.'

'Ring him,' Amber said. 'Ring my father. We have to at least try.'

Randall brought up a large screen in the middle of the room. He entered his brother's mobile number, and the video call symbol came on as the phone rang. It was answered on the first ring.

Amber's father filled the screen. He was in a full suit and tie – the whole shebang – with a view of New York's skyscrapers behind him. He appeared to be in a hotel.

'Hello, Randall,' he said. 'Is Amber okay?'

'Amber's fine, yes, but–'

'Good. I have a meeting in a bit and don't have much time. Maybe I could call you back later?'

'Listen,' Randall said, stopping his brother from hanging up. 'We have something of a situation here.'

'Situation? What situation? Where are you?' Amber's father frowned as he peered into his screen. 'Randall, tell me you're not at Presto! right now, are you?'

'Hi, Father.' Amber gave a nervous wave as she moved into view.

'Amber?' Her father gaped at her. 'Randall, I can't believe you've done the one thing I asked you *not* to do!'

'I'm sorry, but she needed to know. She needed to explore for herself–'

'Please, don't be mad, Father. I love Presto!, and I love Evadne. I'm so glad I came, but we really need your help and it's urgent.'

'If it's anything to do with that place, you already have my answer. Your uncle knows full well that I never want to get mixed up in any of that ever again – and neither should you! Take her home this instant, Randall!'

'That's just it,' Randall cried. 'There won't be a home to get back to if we don't sort things out here. The Wicked Witch has opened a portal that's causing the collision of the Cosmos. If we don't undo the process, both our world and the Hidden Realms are in danger.'

'Please, Father?' Amber pleaded.

Amber's father looked at her for a moment, then, letting out a sigh, he loosened his tie. 'What do I need to do?'

'I have a machine,' Randall said. 'If you can reprogram it, we can fix this whole crazy mess. Come back to Evadne, Andy.'

Amber's father sighed again and pulled up his sleeves, revealing a sparkling pair of cufflinks. 'I guess I always knew you or Onya would need me one day. Luckily for you, and against my better judgement, I had my element embedded into these cufflinks. Let's see if it still works, shall we?' Propping his mobile phone on the table, he flexed his hands and teleportation beams sprung out from the hotel's TV screen.

Moments later, he appeared in the middle of the Presto! workshop. Amber threw herself into his arms. For once, he didn't push her away.

'I'm so glad you're here, Father. I'm so sorry about your sister.'

'I had to tell her,' Randall said quickly.

'I'm sorry that I never said anything. There was just a lot to explain. I didn't know where to start. In the end, it was easier just to be silent,' her father admitted. Amber hugged him tighter. He cleared his throat. 'Now, where's this machine that I'm supposed to reprogram?'

Amber and Randall led him to where the Deus Machina sat, atop the wide trolley, and he perched on a seat that hovered close to the machine.

'Right. Which input codes have you tried so far?'

Amber showed him.

'Ah. Your formula won't synchronise like that. Try this.' He demonstrated a short C++ script. Amber watched the Deus Machina expectantly, but nothing happened.

'Dammit, I thought that would work!' Her father ran his hands through his hair in frustration.

'Show me again,' Amber said.

Her father input the code again. Amber watched

closely. 'Um, how about if we try adding this?' she asked, tapping the keys. Lights flashed in rapid succession on the Deus Machina.

'Amber, that was genius,' her father grinned.

'Like father, like daughter,' Randall winked.

'Enough of the compliments,' Wolf growled. 'There's serious work that needs doing here.'

Taking it in turns, Amber and her father managed to get a workable program running. Soon, they'd rewritten the entire script. The Deus Machina purred into life.

'Yes!' Wolf and Randall cried out at the same time in excitement.

'We did it!' Amber grinned.

Her father's lips curved in a soft smile. 'We sure did.' Hesitating momentarily, he put an arm awkwardly around her. In that moment, Amber saw him as he once was, long ago: Andy the programmer, and an agent of Presto!.

Chapter Twenty-Five

REUNION

Now all they had to do was get the machine to Gran Red's cottage. Wolf took charge of the Deus Machina, carefully tugging the trolley across unsteady pathways, his muscles bulging. The collision of the Cosmos was intensifying and the ground shook, cracking in places. Amber could hear her father and Randall behind her, talking with an ease she would never have thought possible. Gone were the cringey pauses and stiffness. They chatted not only more like brothers, but also as friends. Randall animatedly told his brother about all the changes that had happened in the Hidden Realms since he'd last been there.

'I remember this path well,' her father was saying. 'How many mad dashes across here did we take to Galactica Eireen's place back in the day?'

Randall laughed; the sound mingled oddly with the rumbling of the skies. 'Too many to count. How she never got tired of our wild antics, I'll never know.'

Amber could only imagine how much of a handful they'd been, and poor Gran Red on the receiving end!

'Seems not much has changed,' her father teased. 'Good old chaos-magnet-Randall.'

They finally arrived at Gran Red's cottage. And not a moment too soon. Strong winds whipped against its glass panes and the whole place was engulfed in dismal beams of doom. As the vortex overhead expanded, it blackened the sky, a harbinger of the end that really was creeping nearer and nearer.

Woodcutter Kayne ran to meet them. 'Any luck?' He had to yell to be heard above the high winds and stormy skies.

'We certainly hope so,' Amber's father replied.

'Andy Abeiro?' the Woodcutter cried, eyebrows raised in surprise. 'Is that really you?'

Amber's father grinned. 'Hello, Woodcutter Kayne. Long time, no see!'

Woodcutter Kayne laughed and the two men embraced. *Wow*, Amber thought. This place was certainly bringing the hugs out of her father.

'Let's get this inside,' Randall said, gesturing to the Deus Machina.

They were doing just that, when outside of the gates of the cottage materialised an armoured pair of cyber critters. They loomed tall and bulky, blocking the entrance to the cottage.

'The Wicked Witch has summoned a guard!' Randall shouted.

Amber braced herself for another battle. 'We got

rid of them once before, we can do it again.'

'Hold on.' Wolf stopped her before she could shield-up. 'There may be an easier way. I can save us the time and effort – lead them away.'

They all looked to Wolf, anticipating what he could mean.

'You lot forget what I'm capable of.' Wolf gave a sly smile before flexing his muscles, only this time it wasn't their strength he used. Rather, the flexing increased to a rapid speed – at which point he began to transform. With each flex, Wolf as they knew him slowly morphed into a totally different form. He became an exact replica of the Wicked Witch. It was altogether impressive.

Disguised as Rosina, Wolf was able to divert the cyber critters, ordering them back to the lair they'd come from.

'Great job, Wolf.' Randall congratulated on his return.

'Why didn't you do that before? Back in the Witch's lair?' Amber asked incredulously.

'There were only two of them this time, as

228

opposed to a whole host,' Wolf said. 'Easy!'

Inside the cottage, Gran Red and Red guarded Rosina, who was now slumped in a chair, still tightly bound by the clamping cloak. The twins were trying, without much success, to stop small pieces of furniture from being swallowed up by the vortex above.

Rosina burst out laughing at the sight of the Deus Machina being dragged into the middle of the room. 'You can't possibly think that that thing is going to have any sort of effect, can you? Look around,' she cackled, 'nothing can stop this now!'

'Wanna bet on that, Witch?' Randall said, and promptly flicked on the activator switch. The Deus Machina sprang to life. 'Andy, are you ready?'

Amber's father took a deep breath. 'As I'll ever be.'

'You've got this, Father,' Amber encouraged.

'*We've* got this,' her father said. 'Amber, help me do this.' Not needing to be asked twice, Amber clambered next to her father, and together they launched the sequence. The gamma rays activated

229

and the mirrored bubbles encircling the spherical cylinder began to spin. High-electron laser rays shot directly into the centre of the vortex. Slowly, they began to draw the ends of the vortex together like ginormous electric forceps. The more the rays worked to seal the vortex, the brighter they became. Eventually, they grew into a blinding glare. Everyone in the room was forced to shut their eyes and shield their faces.

Suddenly, a loud *ZAP!* ripped through the air.

The searing flash began to ebb.

Growing dimmer and dimmer, it finally settled into a warm glimmer. Amber opened her eyes just in time to see the glimmer fade and the machine shut down completely. It clanked once, like a final heartbeat, before going dead. A hiss of smoke rose up from its now darkened surface.

There were no more stormy skies. No gale force winds. No earthquakes. Daylight had returned. Shouts of joy and collective sighs of relief were heard across the room. They'd just saved the worlds!

Rosina began to sob.

'Let's get you into custody, shall we,' Woodcutter Kayne said to her. 'You're going away for a very long time.'

The Deus Machina may have been totally fried, but balance and harmony had been restored to the Cosmos. *And to other things as well*, Amber thought, as she watched Randall sling an arm around her father's shoulders.

Woodcutter Kayne gave a small salute to the two brothers. 'Good to see you again, Andy,' he said. 'Hope to see more of you in the future.'

'Good to see you too, old friend. Unfortunately, age is catching up with me more than most. Don't know if I have the stamina to match the pace in these parts.'

'You've more than proved yourself today,' Woodcutter Kayne replied.

Wolf hoisted Rosina up, swinging her over his broad shoulders. Constricted as she was by the clamping cloak, she wouldn't have been able to take a step on her own.

The twins spoke to their stepmother for the first

time since they'd left her in the kitchen, seemingly ages ago.

'We know there was goodness in you; somewhere in all that pretence,' G said to her. 'You could have chosen to let that part win. You could have chosen family.'

'I did it *for* our family,' Rosina said. 'We could have been the greatest, most powerful family in the worlds.'

'You did it for you,' Hans had the same hurt look as his sister. 'You have no idea what a family really is. Goodbye, Rosina,' he said softly.

They watched Wolf and their father escort her away.

Amber felt sympathy for the twins. Although they'd triumphed over the Wicked Witch yet again, there was still a sense of loss. Fake or not, she'd been their mother figure for a long time.

Amber went over to Hans and G. 'Are you guys okay?' she asked.

'Guess we're just grateful her reign of terror has ended.' Hans braved a smile.

G released a breath. 'We're finally free! Think we should head after Father.'

Amber gave a nod.

'And hey,' G went on, 'whenever you find yourself in our woods again, just drop by.'

'Yeah,' Hans agreed. 'We'll show you a move or two for your next Presto! job.' Here, he chopped at the air with precision.

'Gladly!' Amber enthused.

With parting high-fives, the twins followed after Woodcutter Kayne.

Gran Red grinned at the two brothers. 'Why, I never! Rascally Randall and Antsy Andy together again! Get over here, let me have a proper look at you!'

'It's great to still have you with us, Eireen,' Randall said, as he and Amber's father exchanged hugs with Gran Red. She may have been a small elderly lady, but she was strong, squeezing them both tight enough to bring on choked laughs.

'Great to still be here, I'll tell you that!' Gran Red laughed too, releasing the brothers from the bear hug. 'We almost all went *kaput* just then. I imagine I have the heroic efforts of Presto! to thank for saving the day. Business still booming?' She didn't wait for an answer before chattering on. 'I remember when you lot were just wee mischievous things running amok in the Realms.' In the next instant her tone changed, losing the upbeat tempo. 'It's unfortunate though, what happened with your sister. All things considered, she was a good one. You all were.'

'And we were all in awe of the Realms' renowned Galactica Eireen,' Amber's father said.

'Didn't stop you running circles around me, did it!' Gran Red wagged a finger.

The two men grinned, like the playful boys they once were.

As the nostalgic natter went on with the grown-ups, Red said to Amber, 'You're Amber, right?'

Amber nodded. 'Yep, that's me.'

'I just wanted to say thank you for saving me,' he said. 'Seriously.'

'Anytime,' she replied.

'I'm Red, by the way,' he said.

'Oh, I know. Not like you weren't the reason for this whole escapade or anything,' Amber teased.

Red shrugged with a laugh.

'Amber, ready to go back?' Randall called to her.

Amber gave her uncle a thumbs up before turning back to Red. 'See you around. Stay out of trouble.'

'Ooh, now that I can't promise.'

Catching onto their conversation, Randall chirped, 'The famous Red Riding Hood staying out of trouble? Not a chance.'

Amber laughed.

There was one more goodbye for now. Amber, her father and Randall gathered in front of the portal mirror. Amber gave the brothers a bit of space to say their goodbyes first.

'I appreciate you coming out,' Randall said. 'I know it wasn't an easy thing for you.'

'I had to. In spite of everything, this place is still a second home to me. And thank *you* for not giving up on me, or on Onya. There's no one I trust more to find her and bring her home. I have faith in you, little brother.' After tapping Randall's shoulder, Amber's father turned to his daughter. 'And as for you … Impressive. I'm very proud of you.'

Amber hugged her father. She didn't think she'd ever stop hugging him. It might even become their thing.

'See you at home, honey. Think your mother and I will cut this trip short and spend the rest of the spring break as a family.'

Amber grinned. 'That would be awesome!'

With that, her father stepped through the mirror and vanished.

'Why don't you and I close up shop and grab some dinner?' Randall asked Amber. 'How's that for an idea?'

'The best!' Amber couldn't agree more. Her first mission at Presto! Magical Recovery Co. was a done and dusted success. She could certainly eat!

Chapter Twenty-Six

EPILOGUE

The Kakamega rainforest came into view as the bright orange sun began to rise just over the treeline. Amber craned her head out of the pop-top Landcruiser, eager to see more of the glorious landscape they were approaching. They had left their hotel in Nairobi a few hours ago to make it to the rainforest in time to watch its awakening.

Beside her, in the driver's seat, her father was dressed in khaki shorts, a t-shirt and a good pair of hiking boots – same as she was. The week-long trip to her father's homeland of Kenya had been a surprise gift for Amber to celebrate the completion of her entrance exam.

As they neared the thick forests that edged onto the grasslands, Amber thought back to the moment she'd stepped into the exam room only a week before.

In single file, the Regency College hopefuls had walked into the school's main hall. Individual desks and chairs were spaced evenly throughout the large area in preparation for the entrance exam. Amber hadn't felt as self-conscious as she normally did. Since becoming more familiar with her heritage, especially her Grandpa Abeiro's story, she had decided to make some changes in her life. The first thing Amber wanted to work on was her anxiety. Whenever she felt overly anxious, she followed one of the calming exercises she'd learned – focussing on her breathing, slowly counting to ten or thinking of a moment when she overcame the seemingly impossible. Obviously, the first thing on that list was helping to save the world from absolute disaster! She could handle quite a lot, actually, when she thought back to that day! As she had walked into the hall directly behind Katie, Amber hadn't tried to avoid or ignore her former best friend.

'Good luck in there, Katie,' she'd said in a clear voice.

Katie had glanced over her shoulder. For a second, she had looked confused, but then she had smiled cautiously.

'You too, Amber.'

The motion of the Landcruiser coming to a halt brought Amber back to the present moment. Her father smiled at her. 'You okay?'

She gave a nod, jumping out of the car after him. 'Great!'

Her father stood with her in the warm glow of the rising sun, overlooking the marshlands and vibrant green trees as far as the eye could see.

'A little different to Hampstead Heath,' he said.

'A little,' Amber repeated with a chuckle.

They slung on their backpacks and started towards the nearest thicket.

'Your mother has no idea what she's missing!'

'No idea! But she probably wouldn't do too well with the heat and damp.'

Her father laughed. 'No. Not too well, I imagine. And is everything fine with you two? I heard something about you quitting the Young Ladies' Association?'

The Young Ladies' Association was one social club Amber's mother had been dreaming of getting her into practically since birth! When her acceptance finally came, her mother had been thrilled to hand Amber the admittance silver charm bracelet with the letters *YLA* engraved on it. Amber, not so much. And her saying no to the offer hadn't gone down very well.

'All that stuff,' Amber said to her father now. 'It's not me.'

'I get it. Mother will come round, don't worry.

But I see you've kept the bracelet.'

Amber still had the band clipped just beneath the the Angelpyrite Randall had given her in Evadne. 'It *is* a nice bracelet!'

'That made Mother happy, I'm sure.' Amber's father handed her a water bottle. They were now well into the thickness of the rainforest. As the sights and sounds swarmed around her, Amber couldn't think of anything else. Not where things stood between her and her mother, the Young Ladies' Association, getting into Regency College – none of it. The only image in her mind was that of a little boy playing in the damp soil of the forest. That boy being her grandfather, Andrew Abeiro Senior, when he'd found the Angelpyrite gemstone.

She pictured it clearly: him with his friends, darting through the thicket of trees, swatting away at fat, round leaves, the air balmy around them under a hot sun. She could see him crouching in the middle of bushes far taller than he was, catching the glimmer of the jagged gemstone from the corner of his eye and reaching for it – and that was the start of it all.

'Am I going too fast for you?' her father asked, stopping a little way ahead of her.

Amber shook off her daydream. 'Not fast enough!' She picked up pace, running in front of him. She couldn't wait to fully explore – exploring was *her thing* these days!

When they returned to the UK, Amber immediately wanted to share her Kenyan experience with her uncle, as well as news of her final result for the entrance exam. Not long after being home, she hopped into a taxi to Brixton. She stepped out onto the street she'd come to know so well since the first time she was there, the late summer air blowing gently across her face. Particularly on an afternoon as pleasant as this, when luck was on her side and the sun shone bright and warm, the city suburb pulsated.

Children played along kerbsides. Groups of frontline rappers thumped out their next hit demo track. Pensioners sat peacefully on deck chairs, chessboards at the ready. Cliques of mothers rocked pushchairs in animated chatter, the gossip passing between them wild enough to fill the pages of any tabloid newspaper.

Bypassing the bustling activity, Amber crossed the street to Randall's building. She'd texted him on her way over, so he was expecting her. She was surprised, however, that he hadn't come out to meet her, as he normally would have. She'd sent another text message just before she'd arrived, but he hadn't responded to it. No matter, she was here now.

Taking the stairs almost two at a time, she raced up to his apartment, laptop in her backpack. When she reached his floor, she was a little breathless but happy and looking forward to his reaction when she told him about the trip and her results.

A loud clatter followed by a big bang stopped her short. Before she could make head or tail of it, nosy neighbour Bobby popped his head round the corner.

'It's been going on like this for bit now,' he said. 'Mother has asked me to tell the Prof to keep it down, but I'm terrified to even think about what's going on in there.'

Ever since his misadventure in Evadne, Bobby had been much kinder to Amber and her uncle – and he didn't *always* complain about the noise.

Another loud wallop came from behind Randall's door, followed by her uncle's exasperated exclamation. Amber sprang into action. Without pause or even knocking, she threw open the apartment door. Bobby nervously peeked over her shoulder. Both their jaws dropped nearly to the floor at the sight before them.

What could only be described as a ginormous cow charged across the living room, causing all kinds of mayhem while her uncle battled to get a hold of the animal. It was about the size of an armoured tank!

'You have to be joking me,' a wide-eyed Bobby breathed behind Amber.

As the oversized herbivore started to charge for the door, Amber and Bobby quickly side-stepped inside the flat.

'Shut it!' Randall instantly called. 'Shut it, please!'

Amber slammed the door shut just in time. The very large cow turned sharply and started rampaging back towards Randall, who was still trying to get a rope around its thick neck.

'Ah, apologies, Amby,' he gasped. 'You've caught me in a bit of a tizz here. Back from Kenya, eh?' Only Randall could casually engage in conversation while trying to overpower an out-of-control beast.

Amber was speechless.

Randall carried on talking, attempting again to lasso his bovine guest. 'How did the exam go?'

Amber blinked. 'I … er, great.' She tried to speak loudly enough to be heard above the thumping. 'I aced it! I'll be starting at the school this autumn.'

'That's my girl! Excellent – well done, you. Now, if you two could each just grab an end of this rope and we can get this toughie settled.' He tossed the rope at them. 'Don't worry, it's only a calf, shouldn't be too hard!'

A calf? He hadn't just said calf, had he? Amber doubted her own ears. It didn't look like a baby anything to her!

But she and Bobby, given very little choice, did as instructed. Finally, between the three of them, they were able to rein in the animal.

'On to the next Presto! job already?' Amber asked. Completely winded, she leaned against a wall. 'What on earth is this thing?'

'Whatever it is, it's no baby anything!' Bobby exclaimed, saying exactly what Amber had been thinking.

'Oh, but it is,' Randall said, also breathless as he held onto the rope tightly. 'And it's come with a digital note attached to it – from the Farmer of Minerva.'

Amber assumed that Minerva was somewhere in the Hidden Realms.

'Giant Country, they call it,' Randall said. 'Apparently, there's been a hijacking involving some magic beans.'

Giant Country. Cows. Magic beans. Amber put two and two together.

'Let me guess, there's also a beanstalk involved, and perhaps somebody called Jack?'

'This *thing* is from Jack and the Beanstalk?' an agitated Bobby gasped.

Randall smiled, and in that smile, Amber could see another adventure brewing. Presto! Magical Recovery Co. was in business once again.

Acknowledgements

Writing this book has been as magical as the world of Presto! itself. I'm privileged to share that enchantment. May there be as much joy in reading it as there was for me in writing it.

Thank you to the team at Sweet Cherry for your tireless dedication and enthusiasm. You took the jottings of a dreamer and turned them into an actual book. Brilliant Ashley Thorpe, without whom the seeds of this story would not have been sown. Jasmine Dove for being so considerate with the manuscript in its infancy, intuitively refining it. Bubbly Sarah Delmege, bursting with ideas and somehow able to get at what I was trying to communicate before I could even fully formulate it myself. Abdul Thadha for your commitment and making me appreciate the value of simplicity over verbosity.

My fellow writers, the MA in Creative Writing Alumni of 2021/22. Mike McMaster, who created a space full of camaraderie. Véronique Guiberteau Canfrere, my biggest champion, the most ferocious reader and enthusiastic provider of feedback. Rebecca Lambert, for your incredible eye for detail, consistency, and lending moral support. Mathew Bridle: you took time, care and consideration in assessing my rough drafts, giving invaluable pointers. Robin Buzza, our occasional sparring taught me as much about myself as my writing.

Trisha D'hoker, Siobhan Jamison, Patrick Quinn and Sonya Hundal for always being supportive and kind, even in the face of my many writing jitters! Dr Chris Westoby, Dr Karina Lickorish Quinn and Dr Sarah Walton, who guided us on our formative storytelling journey.

My knowledgeable Suffolk mentors Mai Black and Cat Weldon, as well as nurturing community leaders Jenny and Brian Jackwitch. My dear friend Kelly Skhosana, whose sparkling humour lightens any load.

The very special Christopher Gardner for holding me up when I needed it the most. Your patience and understanding are truly remarkable. You kept me sane enough to continue putting pen to paper. I appreciate you so much.

Peter Bayer: I walked into your journalism classes an uncertain young girl with a passion for writing and left a confident young woman who felt that passion was worth sharing.

Finally, my incredible Mum, who made my whole world possible, and my dear boys Sammy and Jonathan – sources of inspiration, spontaneity and fun as only little ones can be.

Take a look at some of our other adventure novels!

A hot summer in Australia brings one young girl face to face with the climate crisis. Luckily, you're never too young to save the world ...

An underground adventure involving robbers, secret passages, old friends — and true courage!

Or, if you're looking for something spooky ...

A charming twist on a beloved gothic tale, a classic villain is turned into the good guy in an adventure that explores modern issues and the balance of right and wrong!

and keep your eye out for ...

COMING 2025!

View the full range at